Jagte Raho

Jagte Raho

Keep Awake

Vishal Akhouri

PARTRIDGE
A Penguin Random House Company

To order additional copies of this book, contact
Partridge India
000 800 10062 62
orders.india@partridgepublishing.com

www.partridgepublishing.com/india

Dedicated to all who belief that life is
indeed a magical experience!

Acknowledgment

I would like to thank my mummy and daddy for all the encouragement they have given me throughout my life.

I would like to thank my sweetheart, my wife Swati, who continues to encourage me to reach greater milestone in my life, and without her my world will not be so much fun and such an awesome fulfilling experience.

To my daughter, Prisha, I would like to say that "You are the cornerstone of our lives and the purpose of our living."

I would like to thank my sister, Meenakshi, who took the pain of reviewing the manuscript and providing her valuable suggestions.

CHAPTER 1

It was 30ᵗʰ December night.

There were joyous festivities in the air. Raghu Dayal was at home in Malviya Nagar, a middle class neighbourhood in South Delhi.

He has got respite from his daily office work for this entire weekend. He planned to take rest lest his friends will allow him to. He knew it will be morning soon and he will have to get up from him slumber to a very cold Delhi morning on the New Year's Eve.

He lived in a two bedroom apartment along with his roommate Rakesh Prakash, whom he has started to dislike more and more lately.

The reason for his dislike was not totally clear to him as well. This was one of those emotions when you start disconnecting with people you have known for long and you try to avoid them and start looking for better people to connect with.

But thankfully for him Rakesh Prakash has gone to his village for a month now. And this has made Raghu Dayal's New Year plans even more delightful.

Poonam Aggarwal, her landlord's daughter whom he had a crush on, was another reason for his delight. His joy was even accentuated when he remembered that he has taken a couple of leaves from office and therefore he was going to have a very long week.

This first week of the New Year he was looking forward to having a lot of enjoyment and fun.

In his reverie, he hoped that this long week never ends. He had to, however, wait for this night to end and he was in no mood of sleeping right away.

He was resting comfortably on the sofa, switching channels on his television and having a sandwich when he heard the night watchman shout, *"jagte raho"* (keep awake in Hindi). He was also banging his wooden stick on the road.

He assured himself of the security of his apartment. But suddenly it descended on him that he has been living in this rented apartment for two years and it is for the first time he has heard a night watchman in the locality.

Moreover, the guards these days don't roam around localities banging sticks on the streets and shouting *"jagte raho"* to ward of any miscreant. This was the practice prevalent with the night watchmen in the early 1980s.

But then he thought this one might be an old school night watchman and chuckled at the thought of it.

He wanted to wake up and have a look outside at this weird guard from him apartment balcony. But his lethargy was not allowing him to get up and walk to the dusty balcony and peek outside in this freezing Delhi night.

Then he though it will be exciting to see this new night watchman and have a quick chat with him. He seems to be the only person awake at this hour of the night apart from him. He decided to move and have a look outside before the watchman turned to some other street.

He came out of his comfy duvet and switched on the night lamp. He was sleeping in the sofa in the living room itself.

He looked around for his sweater and sandals. He put the remote control of his television back near the television set once he managed to find it wrapped and lost in the crevice of his duvet in which he was sleeping. He, however, did not manage to find his cell phone anywhere.

He looked at the clock hanging from the wall. It was 2:15 am at night.

He slowly moved towards the front door of his apartment to have a look outside and to hopefully have a glimpse of this old fashioned night watchman.

As he moved slowly closer towards the front door, he felt a loud shudder on the front door.

He felt it loud enough to wake up a dead man from his grave. *"Dadadadada"* it sounded.

He was scared to the core. He whispered without any confidence, *"Who's there?"*

He heard no reply back from outside the door except for the sounds of cricket hidden in between the cracks of this house and the community park in front of his balcony outside.

Raghu Dayal consoled himself, *"May be that was because of a mild earthquake or a truck passing by."*

But deep within he has already rejected these explanations to be false, before he could have even thought about it.

But then he had no other logical explanation for this weird shudder on the otherwise calm night that he could have accepted reasonably.

He gained courage though and opened the front door.

As Raghu Dayal ventured out he could feel the stillness in the air on the front porch. As he moved towards the Balcony the stillness everywhere was quite evident.

He looked outside the balcony and to his utter shock and disbelief; the area in front of his balcony looked unusually different from what he was used to seeing.

He was standing in front of his own rented apartment where he has been living for two years now and the view from his own balcony looked rather unfamiliar to him.

He pinched himself to confirm if he was dreaming.

He whispered *"Ouch!"*

He was indeed quite awake and the view in front was real. He felt his feet becoming lull at the thought of all these unusual events at this hour of the night.

Suddenly he heard the front door close behind him with a banging sound.

"Dhup!"

He has been a great fan of horror movies, but when things as scary as these happen to us in person, then only do we realise what in reality this feels.

This much anxiety and fear was too much for him to handle and he fainted right there on the cold floor of the front porch.

Raghu Dayal finally woke up late in the morning.

As he gained consciousness, the events of the night flashed back in his memory. He sprung up from his bed and rushed to the front porch.

The front view from his apartment was restored to its usual view.

He could see the neighbourhood park outside with all the familiar people soaking themselves in the December sunshine on this cold winter day. Children were running around in the park.

There were more than normal activities on the street and in the park as he remembered that it was the last day of the year today. And most of the schools were closed for the day on the eve of the New Year.

Suddenly, a hand touched his shoulder from behind.

This caught him by surprise.

The closing of the front door the previous night also flashed back to him. He was expecting a ghost behind him as he immediately turned back.

But it was Poonam Aggarwal, the beautiful daughter of his landlord.

He felt relieved and happy to see her here.

Raghu Dayal had a secret crush on Poonam Aggarwal though he never saw any future there.

He was in his early thirties and was unmarried. She was in her earlier twenties and was still studying. He has never expressed his feeling neither did he intended to do that.

Poonam Aggarwal asked him in her very familiar voice, *"Hey! What happened to you? Hope you are doing alright now!"*

He was happy but at the same time amused to see her here at this time in the morning.

Raghu Dayal sounding a bit puzzled, *"Poonam, you here?"*

Poonam Aggarwal sounding equally puzzled, *"Yes, I came to ask you regarding your roommate in the morning. When I saw you lying on the porch at eight in the morning, I called Papa who helped me put you back in bed."*

"Papa gave you some medication as we thought you might have fallen because of morning chill and we warmed up your room with the heater. What exactly happened to you? Why did you faint on the porch?" enquired Poonam Aggarwal.

Raghu Dayal remembered the night's events; the 'jagte raho' night watchman, the loud shudder at the front door, the unusual view from his familiar balcony and finally the ghostly closing of the front door.

He wanted to think of all of this as a nightmare or a hallucination in case he was dreaming all this with his eyes wide open.

He did not want to let Poonam Aggarwal know this for the fear of scaring her away from him. He decided to make a story.

"Oh yeah! What a cold morning it was. I fainted probably because of last night booze and extreme cold outside" mused Raghu Dayal.

"Thanks for helping me out. For how long have I been unconscious?" asked Raghu Dayal.

"I think for three hours from 8 o'clock in the morning" replied Poonam Aggarwal.

Raghu Dayal recalculated in his mind, *"from 2 at night till 11 o'clock in the morning, nine hours that's a lot of time to remain unconscious."*

But at the same time he was delighted to start his day and the long New Year weekend ahead with a good care from Poonam Aggarwal.

He still had last night's events in his mind but he has started to doubt himself more and more now as he could see everything was normal and there was nothing to be termed as abnormal at the moment.

Poonam Aggarwal bid him farewell and promised to come back to enquire about his health. He had a sweet corner for her in his heart and therefore felt good to have started his day like this after a very unpleasant night.

While still in his reverie he remembered his friends who have not showed up yet. He looked around for his phone and finally found it tucked in the sofa corner of his living room.

There were 29 missed calls in all.

"Oh God!" exclaimed Raghu Dayal.

He started checking the missed call list.

"Mummy", there were six calls.

"Ramu Kaka", there were six calls.

"G. Reddy", there were 6 calls.

"Rohit Shetty", there were 6 calls.

"Riya Kundu", there were 3 calls.

And finally there were 2 calls from unknown numbers. While he has been sleeping his friends and family has been calling him.

First, he called his mother and told her that he overslept and therefore could not receive her call.

Her mother has called to inform him that she was going on two week pilgrimage in Himalayas along with a couple of her neighbours from her home town.

She told her that she will try to call her frequently but her mobile might become unreachable at times. So he should not worry.

Then like a typical Indian mother, rest of her talk was concentrated on persuading his now aging son get married. And equally like a typical Indian son, Raghu Dayal was ignoring most of what she was saying.

She also mentioned that in her absence she will give the keys to her house to one of his friends. His conversation with her mother seemed a waste of time to him. He felt he had more crucial things to sort out this morning.

He was quick to end this call and promised to call her often.

Next, he thought of calling his friends G. Reddy and Rohit Shetty as he has planned to spend this weekend with them.

Chapter 2

While he was thinking of calling G Reddy and Rohit Shetty, his cell phone rang. He checked the display, it was Riya Kundu calling.

"Hello Raghu!" greeted the voice from other end of the phone.

"Riya! Is that you? How are you doing!" enquired Raghu Dayal.

"Yes, that's me Riya Kundu. Hey! I have been trying to reach you since morning" replied Riya Kundu.

"Hey Sorry Riya! I wasn't feeling well since morning"

"And I thought you were trying to avoid me" interrupted Riya Kundu with a bit of a chuckle in her voice.

Raghu Dayal wasn't interested in engaging in street talk with Riya Kundu. Raghu Dayal has never been a great fan of Riya Kundu.

He had more important things in his mind to think about at the moment. He wanted to cut short this conversation with her.

"Riya, I am not feeling well. I got to go now" replied Raghu Dayal in a hurried voice.

"No issues hope you did not have a very bad nightmare. See you soon" Riya Kundu sounded rejected.

Raghu Dayal held the cell phone to his ears for some time as Riya Kundu hung up. Riya Kundu's last words came flashing back *"A very bad nightmare!"*

"How did Riya know about my happenings of the past night? Or was she just being her?"

"Why did she call me three times since morning? But did not spoke anything about that" thought Raghu Dayal.

But given the way Riya Kundu has been behaving with Raghu Dayal, it was not very hard for Raghu Dayal to understand her behaviour.

She has been one of most annoying people in his life seconded only by his roommate whom he has most recently started to dislike even more than Riya.

Raghu Dayal had to bear with her for the simple reason that she was his only friend from nursery school who has managed to maintain contact with him. Both their families were close acquaintances since they lived in the same locality of Shahpur Jat in South Delhi.

However, both the families parted long back as they moved to different localities. And Raghu Dayal was not very sorry to part from the bully Riya Kundu has been.

But recently their lives have crossed again when Riya Kundu joined the same organisation Raghu Dayal worked for.

From whatever memories of his childhood Raghu Dayal could recall, he has never liked Riya Kundu much. He thought of her to be a big bully and very annoying kid.

He must have had such unpleasant time with her that he could not forget and forgive her.

At present, he could not recall the exact incidents but the related bad feelings and emotions are still quite fresh in his mind.

His current strategy towards Riya Kundu was to keep as much distance as he could.

G Reddy and Rohit Shetty would often tease his association with her as that of long lost love. Sometimes even Raghu Dayal would have feelings for her.

Riya Kundu has definitely grown into a beautiful damsel. But for Raghu Dayal her unpleasant reputation was enough to over shadow her attraction. And he would retract to maintain healthy distance from her whenever he felt her attraction growing.

It was turning out to be a lazy day for Raghu Dayal. He was still pondering upon his conversation with Riya Kundu and was trying to figure out in the flow of his conversation with Riya anything that could point out if she already knew about his nightmarish encounter.

He was thinking about all kinds of possibilities.

"May be Riya Kundu as per reputation was just trying to throw familiar slur on him."

"May be she knew about their plan for a grand New Year party and she was trying to find out if she was going to be part of it."

"May be her comment about my nightmare was just one extra statement from a cunning woman."

"Or maybe she knows everything he has been facing and was responsible for it."

But in all possibilities, he knew that Riya Kundu will never answer him directly.

He knew it will not be fruitful to call her back to enquire about what she really meant. He thought it will not be worthwhile thinking any more about it.

He turned his thoughts to the New Year plans that he and his two friends, G Reddy and Rohit Shetty have planned for a long time now.

Raghu Dayal tried calling both G Reddy and Rohit Shetty back but both their phones were unreachable. He tried again but still there was no answer.

Both of them did give Raghu Dayal calls on his mobile phone when he was unconscious but now their phones have gone unreachable. He was getting worried about them.

Raghu Dayal's thoughts were interrupted by a knock on his door. He heard the familiar voice of retired Colonel Pratap greet him before Colonel actually appeared from behind the door.

"Hello Son, how are you doing today?"

"Sorry Raghu, I had to go out in the morning for something important, but all this while I have been thinking about you and your poor health."

Colonel Pratap was Raghu Dayal's landlord and Poonam Aggarwal's father. He retired from Army five years back and was now head of security at a private security agency in south Delhi.

"I did hear Poonam mention that you were cold and hungry and therefore you fainted in the morning."

Raghu Dayal interrupted *"Yes, that's right Colonel Pratap."*

"Hmm, I have seen many lost soldiers die in Siachen glacier on the border because of cold and hunger, son. I seriously doubt it was just hunger and cold. Wouldn't you like to tell me the entire story? I can help."

But Raghu Dayal was too unconvinced himself to let anyone else know about the nights happenings. He feared he might be misunderstood because the night's events were inexplicable.

"There was nothing at all, Colonel Pratap. I would sure let you know if there was anything meaningful happening."

Colonel Pratap though unconvinced said *"Well, fine!"*

While Colonel Pratap began to leave after spending some more time with Raghu Dayal, he stopped him and asked, *"Colonel Pratap! Have we hired a night watchman for our colony recently?"*

Colonel Pratap while making an exit from the apartment replied *"No we don't have one."*

Raghu Dayal was more puzzled now. He was thinking who was that watchman banging his stick on the road and shouting *'jagte raho'* then?

An hour has passed and Raghu Dayal has tried calling his friends G Reddy and Rohit Shetty many times. But their phones have remained unreachable. He was now getting more worried with each passing moment.

And suddenly a phone rang.

"Tring, Tring!"

The tone sounded like an old landline. The ring was coming from his roommate's adjoining room. His heart started pounding because as far as he remembered there was no landline phone in his apartment lest his roommate has kept it hidden from his prying eyes.

He did not move for few seconds to ensure that he wasn't dreaming again. Suddenly the phone bell went silent. He felt happy about that but in a couple of seconds the phone started ringing again.

His heart sank at the sound of each *'tring'*. He moved slowly towards the closed door of his roommate's room. With each step that Ragu Dayal made towards the sound, the shrieking sound was becoming stronger.

He entered his roommate's room to find out that he wasn't dreaming. There was indeed an old black round dial phone on his roommate's side table.

The phone was indeed ringing. He pulled up the receiver and from the other side of the phone receiver, came a sound of an old lady coughing.

She called out *"Bachu!"*

Raghu Dayal's body froze and he could not move his hands either to put the receiver back on the phone holder neither could he reply her back.

The old lady's voice has gone blank and soon there was a long static sound in the receiver.

Raghu Dayal was paying no attention to the static on the phone. The old lady voice was also not in his mind at the moment.

His eyes were stuck on his roommate's bed.

His roommate's body was there on the bed. His eyes closed and blood spurting from his wound right above his heart.

This was a horrible scene.

Raghu Dayal has gone blank with his senses at this sight. He couldn't hold back any more at this ghastly sight. He puked on the floor. His hands and feet were all cold.

He fell on the floor straight on his head and fell unconscious instantly.

CHAPTER 3

Once he woke up, he saw himself in a room that looked like one from yesteryears. He could hear a few kids playing and giggling outside at some distant place.

In the room, he could see lots of old blackened utensils around. Apart from that there was an old bed and a broken chair.

Raghu Dayal felt very claustrophobic in this room. He was lying on the cold floor.

Suddenly he saw the floor collapsing at the rear end of the room. He felt the collapsing floor was moving closely towards him.

He tried to move but he could not. He felt that his legs were glued to the floor. He tried to reach out for the door nearby but his hands felt too heavy to move.

"Help me, help me, save me" He shouted.

He shouted loudly.

He shouted at the top of his voice.

The gapping floor was moving closely towards him. Suddenly he felt the floor move under his feet and he was being sucked inside the collapsing floor.

He was now sinking into an infinitesimally deep sinkhole.

"Nooo!" he shouted as loud as he could.

He has closed his eyes tightly. Suddenly he heard someone running towards him.

As he gained consciousness he opened his eyes. He found himself back in his roommate's room.

He wanted to look at the bed to see if his friend's body was still there or was it taken away for cremation or may be post mortem.

But lying on the floor and unable to move, he was not able to see what was there on the bed clearly.

He heard noises around him. He was not totally conscious yet. He could feel a few people carrying him away. Then he felt being put in an auto rickshaw.

He could hear traffic noise and car horns on the road.

He knew he was being carried somewhere but he did not know exactly where. Neither did he have any clue about who these people were carrying him away and for what purpose.

It felt ages to him in the auto rickshaw.

Meanwhile at his home in Malviya Nagar, Poonam Aggarwal has come to hear from his neighbours that Raghu Dayal has hurt himself in the house, fell unconscious and was carried away to nearby Sachet Max Hospital.

She rushed to Raghu Dayal's house. She wanted to know what happened to him. He has fallen unconscious twice today.

At Raghu Dayal's house, his neighbour Raju Sharma has pulled a chair near his apartment's entrance gate. Raju Sharma has been watching a rather exciting event unfold in this rather dull neighbourhood.

As he saw Poonam Aggarwal coming towards the house, Raju Sharma was excited to tell her the entire story.

He got up from his chair and in high pitched voice started to speak.

"I heard Raghu Dayal shouting loudly. I gathered people and when we went to his room upstairs he was unconscious. I called up the police and the ambulance"

"Thanks a lot" replied Poonam Aggarwal.

"I am going to check the house upstairs. Will you come with me?"

Raju Sharma wasn't expecting this. In a hesitant voice, he replied *"Alright!"*

He followed Poonam Aggarwal as they climbed up the stairs to Raghu Dayal's apartment on the first floor. Inside the apartment, the rooms felt warmer than usual.

The living room in which she has last seen Raghu Dayal was fairly clean. She saw his roommate's room unlocked and entered the room. Raju Sharma followed.

"This is where we found him unconscious" Raju Sharma pointing his finger on the floor.

Poonam Aggarwal examined the room. She could not find anything unusual. She has been there in this room just before Raghu Dayal's roommate left for a month long vacation to his home town.

The bed was tidy with a clean white sheet on it. The single sofa and study table were at its place. However, she saw the side table used to have a vase which has fallen by the side and was broken.

Raghu Dayal's behaviour today was turning into a mystery for Poonam Aggarwal. She liked Raghu Dayal and wanted to help him.

"I think Raghu Dayal has gone mad. You should have heard him shout. I almost fell from my chair hearing him shout" added Raju Sharma.

Poonam Aggarwal kept quiet thinking what could have caused otherwise so sane person shout and behave like a mad man. She had absolutely no idea though at this point of time.

"Poonam, I got to leave now. See you later!" Raju Sharma made his way out of the room hurriedly.

Rumours have been flying high in this close knit neighbourhood that if Raghu Dayal wasn't mad then his apartment must have become haunted with so much happening there in one day.

Raju Sharma was obviously aware of this and did not want to fall prey to any ghost at his old age.

Poonam Aggarwal came out of Raghu Dayal's roommate's room. She sat on the couch in the living area where she has left Raghu Dayal in the morning.

She sat there thinking about it all. She was thinking about Raghu Dayal.

What a nice fellow he has been! But at this moment she knew that the poor fellow was having a bad day. He might have fallen ill and therefore becoming unconscious all the time.

Poonam Aggarwal, however, did not see the real danger Raghu Dayal might be in. His dreams looked very real and for Raghu they were more than mere manifestations of his mind.

Poonam felt assured that he was in the hospital now and the doctors will hopefully take good care of him.

She did not know when she fell asleep on the couch. She woke up around 8 o'clock at night.

It was already dark on the cold 31st December night. She did not have any plans for a New Year party. Her friends at Delhi University have tried to ask her to join but her being the way she was, quite reserved, and has politely rejected the invitation. She wanted to stay at home for her usual quieter new year.

Poonam Aggarwal thought of locking the apartment and leaving a note for Raghu Dayal to collect the pair keys from her in case he did not collect his while being taken to the hospital when he fell unconscious.

Her father Colonel Pratap was not at home tonight and has to go on an assignment, the details of which she had no clue about.

Ever since the death of her mother, Poonam Aggarwal has lived like an orphaned child. Her father has had nothing to do with her life. She has turned into an introvert and a reserved character to the core.

Her father Colonel Pratap who was earlier a great family man found other engagements outside home to keep himself busy.

Poonam Aggarwal did have a few friends at the University but not very close ones.

She was now on her way out of Raghu Dayal's apartment. She started scribbling a note for Raghu Dayal before she locked the door.

She suddenly heard a cell phone ring. She instantly recognised it to be that of Raghu Dayal's mobile phone.

"That poor fellow has left his mobile phone at home."

She quickly opened the door again and frantically started to search for it. She finally found the mobile phone tucked into a sofa pillow.

The call was from an unknown number. She received that call.

"Hello Raghu Dayal, I am G Reddy's father. Raghu did you hear anything from my son today?"

"We have tried to call him since morning but he has not replied back. Can you please help us? We are very worried."

The line went blank after this. Poonam tried calling back but that phone number was unreachable.

Chapter 4

Poonam Aggarwal though not exactly privy to all that has been happening to Raghu Dayal but she was feeling that something unusual was happening around Raghu Dayal. She really wanted to help Raghu.

It was 9 o'clock on 31st December night. She was still in Raghu Dayal's apartment holding his mobile phone in her hand.

She decided to have another look around the apartment. She wanted to find if there was anything unusual that she might have missed till now.

She decided to start with the living room she was in. She has a look around - Television panel, sofas, dining table. She proceeded to Raghu Dayal's bedroom - bed, computer table.

She did not see anything unusual till now.

She then went into his roommate's bedroom. She checked his bed, side table, sofa, computer table. She got no clues of any insanity there as well.

But she was leaving; she saw something on the side wall. It was an old calendar from year 1976 and the month marked there was that of December. As far as she remembered, she has not seen the calendar there.

She was thinking, *"Why would Raghu Dayal's roommate hang a calendar from 1976 in his room?"*

"This was year 2014 which was about to end in about two hours from now."

She decided she had enough of this drama already and decided to leave. She came out of the room into the living area and made her way out of the apartment.

She locked the door behind and left a note for Raghu Dayal tucked to the door handle.

She has mentioned in the note that Raghu Dayal can collect the extra keys from her when he returned from the hospital. There was also a side note mentioning her conversation with G Reddy's father.

Meanwhile at the hospital, Raghu Dayal has found consciousness and was recovering well.

He wanted to inform Poonam Aggarwal, G Reddy, and Rohit Shetty and for some reason Riya Kundu as well about his whereabouts.

He wanted to tell them that he was well now even if he knew none of them would know in the first place what all he was suffering from. But he did not have his mobile phone with him; neither did he remember any of their mobile numbers.

He asked the nurse attending him if he can go home now. He made sure that he explained her that he was feeling absolutely fine now. But the nurse told him that he could be discharged only after the doctor's examination next morning.

Raghu Dayal did not wanted to spend the New Year night in a hospital bed. But at the same time he did not wanted to go to his apartment tonight and to the same nightmares he has been having there.

He knew a place to go to. He wanted to go to G Reddy and Rohit Shetty's shared apartment near 'Shani Mandir' (Saturn Temple) in Noida', a suburb in Delhi.

But the nurses at the Hospital wouldn't let him go out. They were obviously doing their duty well.

But Raghu Dayal was in no mood to comply today. All these events were driving him crazy.

Earlier in the day, he did get it confirmed with the neighbours who helped him out of his roommate's room that he was all alone in the room shouting hysterically.

This was driving him crazy because the naked body of his roommate on the bed looked as real as reality could be. He could still smell the cold blood in his nose just thinking about it.

Resting in the hospital bed for so long and having not much useful things to do, he has tried to recall the events of the day and thinking logically about it to prove to himself that he was not turning crazy. But it was hard to reason out with him that if he was not turning insane, how did the illogical seem so real?

All these looked so paranormal to him! He did not want his mind to roam in that direction. He thought to himself there has to be a logical explanation to all this that is closer to reality. And he was going to find it out.

It was 10 o'clock at night now. He was getting more and more restless and wanted to get to the bottom of this.

He thought he might visit a good psychologist who may be able to find some meaning in all these hallucinations.

He needed to be consoled and told that he was not turning mad. He needed his friends G Reddy and Rohit Shetty around him. He felt alone in this hospital bed. He really needed people around him whom he could tell his story to and not be mocked about it.

With all this craziness, he decided he was not going to stay in this hospital and probably declared mad by the doctors the next day and be shifted to a permanent asylum where he would spend the rest of his life.

He soon found himself out of the hospital bed with the little trick he had to play on the nurses and ward boys who were on night duty in emergency ward of the hospital.

His trick of putting pillows and covering it with a bed sheet was too lame though and soon the hospital guards were alerted.

They found him in the parking lot.

As he saw the guards coming towards him, he ran towards the city road. He was still in his hospital ward suit and he felt really cold and stupid that he did not have the mind to wear a jacket before he made his unwanted escape.

He was sure as he looked back on his crazy escape that he will surely be termed as mentally ill when his report will be prepared by hospital authorities tomorrow.

He at one time thought of giving up running and return back to his cosy hospital bed and in the process gain some of his lost reputation back.

Suddenly he got the chills as he felt that although the hospital guards had abandoned the chase but a black car was speeding right towards him with full intension to hit him hard and hurl him a few feet in the air.

He made an instant decision not to enter the empty stretch of the road and crazily decided to jump towards the wrong side of the traffic.

As he was about to do that a white Honda city car from the other side of the road turned around. A familiar voice shouted *"Raghu! Get inside the car now!"*

Raghu Dayal jumped inside the white Honda city car. He could see the black SUV on the other side of the road stop instantly.

His doubts were confirmed that whoever was there inside the car wasn't Raghu Dayal's friend. As he gained his breadth, he saw Riya Kundu behind the car steering. He has never felt so relieved and happy seeing her.

"Riya, thanks a lot for saving me" said Raghu Dayal politely.

"But how come you are here at this time?" asked Raghu Dayal looking puzzled.

"Raghu, I came to visit you when I heard about you being admitted in this hospital" replied Riya Kundu.

"Visit me at this time? What time is it now?" Raghu Dayal asked looking puzzled.

"It's 11:15 now" was Riya Kundu's reply.

Although Raghu Dayal was not satisfied with the answer but he knew this is the best he could have got from her.

She sped past 'Rai Pithora's Fort' and took a turn towards Mehrauli. She crossed the historic 'Qutab Minar' on her way.

"Where are we going?" asked Raghu Dayal.

"To somewhere warm and safe, my father has a farmhouse in Chattarpur (a locality in South Delhi)."

"Can we go to my apartment instead?"

"I doubt you would want to go to your apartment now after all this that you have faced there."

"How do you know about all that has been happening to me Riya?"

"I will tell you all that but first you must tell me all that has been happening to you."

"Riya Kundu! You know that I don't trust you much."

"Raghu Dayal! If anyone has lost all his trust it's you."

"Raghu, now tell me. Do you know where G Reddy and Rohit Shetty are at this moment?"

"No, I don't know but why do you ask?" Raghu Dayal tried to be as casual as he could with his answer but he himself was very worried about his friends.

"Raghu Dayal, what have you been doing with your mind!"

"Excuse me! Will you please tell me what's going on?"

"Raghu! I doubt if you don't know this but G Reddy is officially missing. I don't know about Rohit Shetty, where he might be; whether missing or hiding."

"Hiding from whom!"

"Do you remember where do they live?"

"Yes, near Shani Mandir (Saturn temple) in NOIDA."

Riya Kundu stopped in front of a heavy gate of the farmhouse which was lined with eucalyptus trees. As the automatic gates opened, she drove in and parked her car inside the affluent farmhouse.

CHAPTER 5

Raghu Dayal got out of the car and stood in front of the farmhouse looking at the posh habitat. He looked visibly impressed at such grandeur.

He did not know that Kundu's father was so rich. There were electric fences all around the farmhouse. The house was all white just like a dream. There was a swimming pool and a fish pond just outside the white building.

Riya Kundu led him inside the house. Inside, it was all white. She asked him to wait on the sofa which was white leather. Raghu Dayal was thrilled to see such opulence and richness from his own naked eyes.

The house was a change from an unusual and bad day he had. He checked the clock on the wall. It was 11:30 at night.

He remembered that in next 30 minutes it will be a new year for the world.

But suddenly he realised that they were not alone in the house. There was some music coming from the backyard of the house. He decided to have a look around to find out. As he went outside towards the backyard, the music and the noise became louder.

There was a party going on in the farmhouse.

A New Year party to welcome the New Year!

Suddenly Raghu Dayal remembered that he had planned to be part of such a party along with his two dear friends G Reddy and Rohit Shetty.

How can he forget this? He did not remember the venue of top of his mind. Probably it was this same party he was supposed to be in. All this day's events have been very hard on his. He needed to relax a bit.

He entered the party from a separation in the otherwise enclosed space in the green lawns. Not a great way to gate crash in the party he thought. A waiter gave him a cold look while he entered.

The disc jockey has taken the centre stage. He was mixing Punjabi and Bollywood songs to the uproar of the guests who were mostly boozed out.

A beautiful girl approached Raghu Dayal, *"Nice hospital outfit!"* She complimented not realising that Raghu Dayal has just run out of a real hospital.

Raghu Dayal came to his senses realising where exactly he has been before this party. He decided to make a quick exit to avoid any further attention.

He choose the same place to the make the exit. And this time there were no waiters to embarrass him.

He decided to go to the same front room where Riya Kundu has asked him to wait.

On his way back he was thinking of what Riya Kundu has told him about this place.

"Is this really Riya Kundu's father's farmhouse? Or was she just joking to him! Nahh no way" he thought.

At the same time, Raghu Dayal's mind was boggling with curiosities one of the latest one being why did Riya Kundu bring him here. He has now fully gained consciousness and was not feeling nauseated by the drugs he had to consume at the hospital.

He knew exactly where he was now and what exactly has been happening to him all day. He was feeling very light in his head, away from any tension or presumptions.

His hallucinations still felt too real to dismiss them as dreams. He was thinking why the floodgates of all these weird hallucinations have opened today only?

He was now more ready to accept the idea that something unnatural was happening around him. All these could not be mere coincidences.

As he was drooling over it suddenly he felt like time slowing down around him. He could feel the freeze. There was complete silence suddenly. No wind was blowing. That felt very scary to him.

He knew that another of weird incidents was coming his way right now. But this time he was ready for it. He has made up his mind that however scary the coming incident might be but he was going to make sure that he did not lose his mind and would remain conscious.

He was ready for whatever was coming his way this time. He was going to use this opportunity to find out why this was happening to him.

The weird incident has already started. He was feeling as if he was in hyperspace. He felt that he was walking in a jar of Petri dish. He was looking at a frozen frame of time. Everything living or dead seemed to have stopped moving except him. His movement was also restricted like walking inside a thick liquid.

He saw a fly near him motionless in air. He went close enough to the fly to look directly in the eyes of this otherwise fast moving fly.

He went towards the fish pond. Even the ripples made by the swimming fishes have frozen. There were few water drops in the air hanging in eternity. This was like a wonderland feeling.

He entered the main hall of the white house where he was sitting initially. The front gate to this main hall was wide open. The lights were dimmed in the main hall. The view he saw there was unbelievable.

Riya Kundu was right there in front of him. He had a revolver in her hand. The revolver was pointed however at another direction. He looked in that direction.

There was another man in the shadows. The bullet has already been fired but has not reached the man in the shadows yet. The bullet was frozen in air just like any other object in this frozen timeframe.

He could move around and touch the released bullet. As he saw the firecracker burst outside in another frozen frame of time, he saw the man in the shadow for the first time.

It was Raghu Dayal himself!

CHAPTER 6

Raghu Dayal, himself, was the man in the shadows.

It was unbelievable and frightening sight for Raghu to view his own death on his face. With a blink of his eyelids, he was back in his time. He was still there in the same hall of the farmhouse. He was alive and not shot by any flying bullet. There was stillness in the air as he tried to gasp his breadth back. There was no Riya Kundu in sight holding the revolver. The main hall door was closed and he could hear the sound of the New Year festivities in the background.

The big clock in the hall was showing time as 11:55 p.m. There was still five minutes to go for the New Year to usher in his life. Suddenly his reverie flashed back and he remembered that the bullet was shot at him when the crackers burst at 12 o' clock. This thought gave him chills.

Is he going to get shot by Raghu Kundu as he has seen in his divine moment? And where was Riya Kundu? He was about to find that out in less than five minutes, he thought.

Just in time at that very moment Riya Kundu appeared in the main hall. She had a revolver in her hand. His reverie was turning into a reality.

Raghu knew for sure that this time he wasn't dreaming. He could feel his heart pounding and sweat racing down his brow on this wintery New Year night.

He was going to be shot dead in less than five minutes!

This was his immediate though. This was very frightening and out of this extreme fear his legs started to become very heavy.

"What are you up to this time?" Shouted Riya Kundu with her revolver pointed directly at Raghu Dayal.

"You have already killed G Reddy and your roommate. And I am not sure what you did with your friend Rohit Shetty. But I know I am your real target. I have always been. Isn't it?"

"You have always kept quiet about this. But today you speak up or you are dead"

The clock struck 12 that very moment. There was a burst of lightening as a fire cracker burst that very moment. That illuminated his face.

He knew exactly what he wanted to do now. He wasted no time. He jumped and ducked behind the sofa in the direction opposite to where he knew the bullet will hit him.

But thud! There was no bullet sound. Raghu Dayal was too scared to realise this. He was begging for mercy and was breathing heavily.

"Riya! Please don't kill me!"

By this time the front door has sprung open with strong wind gushing in. The setting was perfect as he has actually seen earlier.

Riya Kundu with her gun aiming and her hairs blowing stylishly to the side was looking more like Lara Croft, the tomb raider and not exactly any murderer whom Raghu Dayal now was imagining to be responsible for all these misfortunes.

But Raghu was too scared to come out from his hideout. He has ducked behind the sofa and did not have any courage left in his heart to even lookup.

He kept screaming *"Riya, please don't kill me."*

Riya Kundu has not expected such a lame reaction from Raghu Dayal. She went closer to him.

"Raghu, what are you doing? Get out of that place now." She commanded.

Raghu Dayal was now shivering with fear. Riya Kundu had a hard time dragging him from behind his hideout on to the sofa.

"Raghu, don't be a pussy!"

"Raghu, now tell me the truth. Speak up. Why did you kill G Reddy and your roommate and where is Rohit Shetty now?"

"Why are you doing all this? Do you have a plan to kill me as well? Why?"

As Raghu Dayal gained his self, he started to listen and understand what exactly Riya Kundu was alleging.

"What! My dear friend G Reddy is dead?"

Riya interjected *"Don't lie to me. Tell me truth. Police have you as the prime suspect."*

Raghu Dayal had to tell Riya Kundu about her hallucinations now.

"Riya, I did see my roommate's dead body in his room. But that I now know was just one of the hallucinations I had been having today. And that is the reason I had the nervous attack and was admitted to the hospital."

"What! You say you had hallucinations of your dead roommate in bed!"

Riya Kundu was shocked to hear this one.

"Riya, I am innocent. I have been trying to call my friends since I haven't heard from them since morning. And why will I want to kill you. I am a normal man and not a serial killer."

Riya Kundu was now feeling pity at the way Raghu Dayal has responded to her threat. She was happy that she has not put any bullets in the revolver and killed him.

Raghu Dayal was still in a state of shock and fear. He was also in tears for the news of the probable death of his dear friend G Reddy and his roommate.

How dearly he was attached with G Reddy and Rohit Shetty only he knew! Riya Kundu had no clue that they were more like brothers and no one would think of even hurting each other forget killing.

Raghu Dayal wanted to know the entire story. But first he needed to catch his breath and get fresh air. He was totally awed at what was happening to himself.

His 31st December has been anything but truly a mishap. And only he knew how he has felt the entire day. He needed to know the answers to his questions and then only will his life turn to normal again.

He realised that he was still inside the hall on the sofa in a very uncomfortable position. He got up from there which alerted Riya Kundu.

Raghu Dayal realising what he has done tried to calm Riya Kundu.

"Riya, I need to catch fresh air outside. Please."

Raghu Dayal sounded low.

She did not say anything neither did she give any negative signal of un-approval.

"I won't go outside the farmhouse."

She finally nodded 'yes' but kept a closed eye on him as he moved outside in the cool breeze that was blowing now and was very soothing.

He needed time to recollect and regroup his thought in order to be successful at drawing any logical conclusion from these rather illogical events that has been happening to him.

He knew he will have to dig the grave himself to find out the truth behind these events. No one from outside can help him; although, he wouldn't mind someone coming out of thin air and explaining him. He wouldn't mind being told that he was the chosen one to face all the miseries in life if that has some logic to it.

He recollected his first sighting and the second one. Both of these were very illogical and unreal. But his last one with Riya Kundu turned out to be a glance in the future.

He was thinking if he has really gained some supernatural power. Has he gained the power to see the future? Or was it another of his dreams that has manifested into a reality.

One thing about the last event bogged him. It wasn't exactly the same as he has day dreamt it. Riya Kundu decided not to have a bullet in his revolver when she came banging on him in a true revengeful attitude.

Did he influence her decision with a lucky foresight? How can the situation turn so paranormal in a matter of one day if this was true?

These were the questions he desperately needed answers for.

He saw Riya Kundu coming towards him. He waited for her because some these she also needed to be asked.

"Are you calm now?" enquired Riya Kundu.

"Yes Riya. You have no idea how tough this 31st December day has been on me. And to top it all to start the New Year with a gun on my head and to be blamed for murder of two men, one of them being my bro G Reddy was too harsh on me." replied Raghu Dayal in a very pensive voice.

"I am still clueless why all this is happening to me. But in order to find the truth we must have faith on each other."

"Do you believe me Riya, that I am a victim myself and not the perpetrator of any crime."

Riya Kundu kept quite in the dull night. A cool breeze was blowing. It blew her hair onto her face. She used her hands to get her hairs to block her view.

"Raghu, it's not just me who doesn't believe you, even the Delhi police is after you. If you are not responsible for all these murders, you will need to prove yourself not guilty of these murders. Also you will need to find where Rohit Shetty is now!"

Raghu Dayal's head has started spinning at the thought of being blamed for these two murders, one of them being his dear friend. He was fugitive now and if he did not do something fast he might be in Tihar jail soon.

All his dreams of the future, his job, his life will be jeopardised.

He knew he will need all the strength in the world to come out a winner in this this most demanding situation of his life. But first he needed to verify all that Riya Kundu has told him. He had to go to his Malviya Nagar apartment.

His strength was giving way though he needed some sleep desperately. But if he waited till tomorrow morning and if whatever Riya Kundu has told him was true, he might be in tomorrow's news as a fugitive. He will then have time only to hide and run.

He needed to act fast tonight only. He also needed Riya Kundu to be by his side to be his alibi in case some more events happened and he be linked to them as well.

He asked Riya Kundu to drive him to his apartment in Malviya Nagar. It was a quiet 30 minutes' drive from the farmhouse to his apartment. As he reached there, Raghu Dayal's heart sank as he saw a group of police vans around his home lane.

Riya Kundu was right, he indeed was a fugitive. Riya Kundu did not stop there and sped past his house lane.

Raghu Dayal asked her to take a right turn on the next street. He wanted to check if Poonam Aggarwal's house also had police stationed. As Riya Kundu drove near Poonam's house, a police van drove past them. Raghu Dayal ducked forwards so as to hide himself but. It was too late.

The police van stopped immediately just a few meters away. Raghu Dayal's heart started pounding heavily.

Was he going to suffer life's biggest humiliation today? Was he going to get arrested on a New Year night? All these thoughts were going in his mind now.

Riya Kundu was quick enough though. She took the immediate left and sped fast, followed by an immediate right.

There was police siren sound behind them although the police van was not visible. Riya Kundu took some more turns in the meandering streets of Malviya Nagar. She stopped her white Honda city on a street where a few other cars were parked.

They got out of the car and walked towards the nearby park ensuring that no one saw them. They sat on a bench in the park and kept a watch on their car in case police van came and found it. They were not alone in the park. There was a couple taking a stroll to welcome the New Year at midnight. There were also few teenagers who were having a party in the park under the night sky.

"Raghu! Is that you?" a voice from behind them whispered to him.

Raghu Dayal shrieked with fear of getting caught. He turned around in anxiety and from the darkness emerged Poonam Aggarwal.

They did not realise in their attempt to dodge the police that they have done a full circle of the streets and they have parked their car right in front of Poonam Aggarwal's house. Poonam Aggarwal has seen them doing that and has followed them in the park to have a word with Raghu Dayal.

As they realised this, there was a lighter mood in the air at least for some time. They were even thinking that the police may not have been following them.

"What the heck!" said Raghu Dayal in amusement and with excitement at the change of luck.

He wanted to talk more but Poonam Aggarwal interjected and asked them to follow her. She took them to her house from the backdoor. Raghu Dayal was familiar with her house and was delighted to be there on the New Year's night. He always has dreamt to be there with her but in obviously more romantic situation than this. But right now his situation was very grave and demanding.

They seated themselves in the dining chairs and gulped a few glasses of water before anyone of them began to speak. There were just questions on their mind. They had no answers. The answer to these would change Raghu Dayal's fate for the good they hoped.

There was unfamiliar silence in the room considering that they had so much going on in their mind and there was so much to talk about. Time was fast running away.

Finally Poonam Aggarwal broke the silence.

"Raghu Dayal, police has been searching your apartment and were looking for you. They think that you are responsible for the murder of G Reddy and your roommate."

"I know that cannot be true. They have been enquiring about you from the entire neighbourhood. There is a constable keeping an eye at your house 24x7."

Whatever Riya Kundu has said got validated. Raghu Dayal's heart sank as he realised that he was indeed in a very bad situation. He has hoped that all that Riya Kundu has been telling him would turn false. But here was Poonam Aggarwal his trusted sweet heart telling him that he was indeed a fugitive.

He couldn't understand how he could have landed in such a deep mess. There was no fault of his that he could recollect.

His mind was occupied with fear and sadness of indeed losing his beloved friend G Reddy.

He could not stop tears from rolling down his cheeks in front of these two ladies. This was turning out to be the worst New Year night as his mood and spirit gloomed with each passing second.

He was thinking that there was no hope for him now. He could imagine himself face to face with G Reddy and his roommate's old parents being blamed for the murder of their young sons. The bread earners of their respective families slaughtered by this merciless Raghu Dayal would be the allegation from the criminal attorney.

He could imagine the whole world turn against him. He would finally be labelled as a serial killer. Then even Poonam Aggarwal might not believe his stories and his real life hallucinations.

He was woken from his gloomy thought by a police siren sound probably from the police van parked outside the house. He had two choices with him.

He could surrender right now and let the police and the lawyers do the talking in the court. And probably his lawyers would be smart enough and prove him innocent to the world.

At this time he thought that given the complicacy of the situation, the lawyers with the best of his intension might not be able to do much to prove that he was not guilty.

The second choice was to be on the run and find out some logic in his hallucinations and the reality around him.

He had already decided and wasting no further time he was sitting alongside Riya Kundu in her white Honda city car and Riya Kundu was already on the road.

CHAPTER 7

They were already speeding away from their last destination. It was early morning now. Light of the morning sun has started to descend from the east. He recalled that it was still the first day of the year. There were people on the road celebrating the New Year this early in the morning, probably going back home after night long party.

Raghu Dayal was happy that at least these two ladies believed that he was not guilty. He now needed to know if he had anyone else who would believe him. His office was closed for the new year long weekend but once it opens again he will have no way to hide from the negative publicity and the consequences of that. The consequences would be far more than he could think of.

Riya Kundu worked with him and she as well was mindful of the consequences. On the face of it, he has murdered two people and was probably responsible for a third one who has been declared missing for now.

They both worked for a secret organisation dealing with the consciousness. Riya Kundu was picked up by the organisation much before Raghu Dayal. She has learned the art in her trade very early.

Raghu Dayal has been recently picked by the organisation. He has turned to be very resourceful and talented pick but at the same time he was immature and unpredictable as well. After the last few assignments, Raghu Dayal has become volatile as well and has lost his original mind completely.

With the current situation Raghu Dayal was in, she will need to go into his mind to find out what exactly was happening and what reality has he created with his powerful mind.

But firstly, Riya Kundu needed to take expert advice and that's where she planned to go next. She knew that she cannot tell all this directly to Raghu Dayal as he might panic and therefore she wanted to gain his confidence and trust.

She knew that his mind was strong enough to capture vibes coming from other people as well and therefore she must forbid herself giving away her intension. She has managed to hide her mind till now successfully from Raghu Dayal. But for how long will this work she didn't knew?

Riya Kundu has on a few previous occasions been in the same assignment with Raghu Dayal where they have worked together. They have been in the minds of people and have successfully executed what they were meant to do.

She knew Raghu Dayal was one of the most talented associates she has worked with. But in almost all assignments he has turned volatile. He would sometimes pick up cues from others mind which would become hard for him to forget and would take days to gain his perspective back. And this is what has happened here as well.

This time though the clues looked very sinister to her. She wanted others in the organisation to feel the vibes and give a more holistic analysis and interpretation of the vibes.

She believed the future of humanity depended on this and there was no scope of taking any chances this time.

Riya Kundu was driving the car towards the historic 'Chandni Chowk'. Their organisation had a safe house there. As they fast approached their destination, Raghu Dayal started feeling more uncomfortable. He started getting strange sensations which got stronger with each passing second.

Raghu Dayal now had a mind of his own which was not exactly what he really was. He had to get out of here. But he was riding in a fast moving car. He needed to think fast and quick. He must engage Riya Kundu in a conversation first.

"Riya! Do you know what we work for and why we do what we do?"

"Of course! And do you remember as well?" Riya Kundu enquired back.

"No, I have kind of forgotten. Somehow cannot recall anything. I don't know what is happening to me"

"Really! This has happened to you third time now. Raghu, you need to concentrate more."

"You are our organisation's top asset. I am just here to guard and support you." Riya knew that it was time Raghu Dayal be brought to his senses.

"Oh! What do you mean by that? What exactly do I do?"

"Raghu! You don't have to ask me! You just have to get in my mind to find out."

She continued speaking.

"Raghu, you are one of our rare few whose left and right brain is totally and equally developed. Your mind is powerful enough to connect seamlessly to the universal mind and therefore you can get in the minds of anyone, and find out the seen and unseen."

Raghu Dayal looked puzzled. Riya Dayal tried to explain this further like a learned teacher.

"Raghu, universal mind is the one we sometimes represent as god. If anyone is able to get in the same frequency as it and be able to talk to it, he will become most powerful. He will be able to influence world opinion."

She took a brief pause to recollect her ideas.

"Every person is sub consciously connected to the universal mind. This is the prime source of our thinking. Thinking and imagination is what creates the world around us. Any person who is able to talk to the universal mind and provide feedback consciously and not just subconsciously is bound to have a very deep influence on the world."

"People who know this are the most powerful people in this world. They have created world opinion and are still remembered after death. People use different techniques to achieve this extreme purpose and pleasure. Some meditate to enter that state. Some groups harness the power of mind of a group for the collective purpose. But with regards to you, you are a gifted soul."

"This is your strength and a curse as well."

Riya Kundu was thinking, *"How many times do I need to tell Raghu his gifted powers!"*

Raghu Dayal seemed to be like the Hindu God *'Hanuman'* who had to be reminded his strengths because he was cursed to forget it.

This was part of the job for Riya Kundu to save her asset. She knew Raghu Dayal was a very special asset indeed and she was chosen to protect him.

But the current vibes that Raghu Dayal was getting, Riya Kundu was not very sure about its origin and its meaning. She wasn't an expert at that but she could sense that this time things were very different. What worried her even more was that Raghu Dayal didn't seem to be in control at all. His state of mind was very volatile.

CHAPTER 8

Raghu Dayal listened calmly to all that Riya Kundu was telling him but he was in a completely different state of mind to comprehend it and react to it. Somehow he did not felt secure in the car with Riya Kundu.

He needed to move out quickly. He did not waste a moment once he has decided. He unlocked the car door and jumped out of the speeding car. But somehow his reflexes were so agile that he did not hurt himself at all. He did not even have a single scratch or any bruises in the process.

Riya Kundu was awestruck at the Raghu Dayal's brevity. It looked to Riya Kundu who watched him escape helplessly as if Raghu Dayal knew exactly how the others car drivers would react at his stupidity. He seemed to know even where the tiniest pebble was placed on the road.

Raghu Dayal seemed to have finally rediscovered himself. Riya Kundu knew that was good as well as bad for her. She needed to find him quickly again. Raghu Dayal in the meanwhile was running away towards the small crowd of people in the nearby marketplace. She could do nothing but watch him disappear.

She decided to drive away and decide on her next course of action. But there was a big banging sound. A truck coming from the other side has hit the road divider. Before Riya Kundu could react to this new threat, the truck crashed into Riya Kundu's car. Her car was hurled three feet in the air.

Riya Kundu could only guess why Raghu Dayal may have made such an insane looking escape before her eyes closed.

There was mayhem on that busy road intersection now. Apart from Riya Kundu car, the truck has hit a few more cars. Some of the accident victims were thrown on the concrete road and there was a lot of blood on the road.

Riya Kundu was still wrapped to the seat belt and the impact has blown the airbag right in front of her open. She has fallen unconscious and will need immediate medical attention if she was to survive this accident.

CHAPTER 9

Meanwhile not far away from the scene of this accident, Poonam Aggarwal's father retired Colonel Pratap was back home. He enquired, *"what is going on with Raghu Dayal?"*

She told him all that she knew.

"Police is after Raghu for the murder of his friend and his roommate."

"What! Don't tell me. You did not inform me. He doesn't look that kind of a bloke. He was a nice calm boy for the two years he has stayed at our place."

"Poonam did the police interrogate you as well."

"*Yes, they did. I told them all I knew. I told about the morning incident when he fainted and also the afternoon one when he fainted and had to be hospitalised.*"

"*Hospitalised?*"

"*Yes. Also he came to our house after midnight along with her friend Riya Kundu.*"

"*What, he came here even when the police was after him. He must be crazy.*"

"*Yes, he was acting weird. They parked their car right in front of our house and were sitting in our neighbourhood park.*"

"*I did not inform the police about this though.*"

"*Do you think Raghu is guilty? I think he is being framed. We should help him. What do you say daddy?*"

"*Yeah, I think the same. Is his house open at the moment? May be we can have a look there and find something to prove his innocence.*"

"*No daddy! His appartment is locked. But wait I have his mobile phone with me. I picked this when I last went there. I forgot to give it to him when he came here in the midnight.*"

"*That is great Poonam. Show me that phone.*"

She placed the mobile phone in Colonel Pratap's hand.

"Poonam, this one is discharged. Don't worry I will charge it now."

They now waited eagerly for the phone to charge up and come to life again.

CHAPTER 10

Meanwhile in another part of the city, Raghu Dayal has already caught Delhi Metro at Karol bagh and was heading towards the Delhi suburb, NOIDA. He intended to find out where exactly Rohit Shetty was in case his other friend G Reddy was actually dead.

It was already midday now. Delhi was bustling with festivities on this first day of the New Year. He had just one thing in his mind that was to find out where his friends were. Thus he may be able to join the missing chain of all that has been happenings to him since the 31st December and find some logic back in his life. He was oblivious of the happy and gay mood around.

As he thought about Riya Kundu, he got worried for her as well although he had no clue that she had a major accident.

But his vibes from her were not good. He was hoping that she was not doing that bad.

He also felt that he should not have made such an escape from her car and rather informed and got out decently. But he did not seem to be in control of his thoughts and action during that one minute of his escape. He seemed to be in auto pilot mode at that time without any control on his actions.

In the metro train, he could feel a lot of chatter. He felt a natural urge to concentrate and listen. He started to scan every feeble voice around. He felt he could also hear sounds which were unsaid. He did not understand where these untold sounds were coming from but they were growing in strength.

As his concentration grew, there was more order and lesser chaos. Soon he knew every person in the train. He even knew exactly where each of them was about to get down. He had a smile of satisfaction in his heart. There was no negative feeling but pure love for every one of his co-passengers.

He gave a smile to a little girl seated next to him and gave her his googles.

"I know you want this" as he moved confidently out of the metro train at NOIDA Botanical garden station.

Raghu Dayal was now headed towards the 'Shani Mandir' (Saturn temple) on the Greater NOIDA expressway. He hired an auto rickshaw for the ride. He was going towards the building where G Reddy and Rohit Shetty lived near 'Shani Mandir'. That was the place he has last seen them together alive.

As the auto rickshaw took the turn to the service lane towards 'Shani Mandir', Raghu Dayal started getting vibes he could not comprehend. He has become more and more anxious as they approached their destination. He was precipitating on a cool January Delhi chill.

Rickshaw driver saw his deteriorating condition in his rear view mirror and asked, *"Sahib! What happened? Are you alright?"*

Raghu Dayal murmured, *"No, I am not alright. Can you please stop the rickshaw right now?"*

The auto rickshaw driver was unusually friendly person; he stopped and asked him, "Do you want some water? Shall I take you to the nearby Jaypee Hospital?"

But Raghu Dayal was too engrossed in seeing the façade of the 'Shani Mandir' that was right there in front of him to listen to what the auto rickshaw driver was saying.

He quietly left the auto rickshaw without even bothering to take the change back from the driver.

It was evening now and soon it was going to be dark. The first day of the New Year was about to end in few hours.

As he moved towards the 'Shani Mandir', the discomfort he felt while travelling in the auto rickshaw was easing out. The smell of the burning 'agarbatti' sticks was getting stronger. The pungent smell of mustard oil which is used in these temples was overwhelming him.

He remembered that G Reddy and Rohit Shetty lived in a building just near this place. He now remembered clearly having spent endless night in this apartment along with his friends. He could recall clearly all the fun they had just a month ago when they last spent their time together. His eyes dampened at the thought that G Reddy was no more. His spirit and his mood became very gloomy at this thought. He wanted to cry out and let his deep emotions to be shown to the world.

He would have in fact probably cried out to vent out his grief but there was something more weird that was getting his attention now.

He seemed to have forgotten the way to his friends' place. He moved around 'Shani Mandir' and could not locate the building. The whole place seems to have been changed and rebuilt in a matter of a day. His head started spinning at this thought.

Was it another of the weird hallucinations he has been having all this time at regular intervals?

He asked a few people but none of them seemed to know the type of the building he was describing to them.

There were a few houses there but none of them resembled what he has described to locals there. The sudden disappearance of the apartment block was driving him crazy again. He knew the house was always there, right there in front of his eyes. Even locals who have lived there for around ten years could not recall the building he tried to describe to them.

He got frustrated with all this. His only hope of finding his friends has vanished with the disappearance of their building itself. Then he saw the 'Shani Mandir', it was still there as he has imagined. It was right there if front of him.

This meant his mind was not going crazy. He has found the 'Shani Mandir', so as per his memory the building he was looking for must be around. He entered the 'Shani Mandir' in search of some quiet place to concentrate on his thoughts.

CHAPTER 11

Meanwhile at Poonam Aggarwal's house, colonel Pratap has just woken from his evening nap. He saw that Raghu Dayal's mobile phone was fully charged now. He switched it on.

The phone came alive with familiar Nokia tune greeting colonel Pratap. He had an anxious look on his face. He held the phone in his palm and let the initial start setup routine to complete.

As the phone came in the mobile network, there were a couple of beeps to indicate the missed calls intimations and smses being delivered. Poonam Aggarwal joined his father in the living room. They had a curiosity of a juvenile at this moment. They had already considered Raghu Dayal not guilty of any crimes. They were therefore looking for clues to prove his innocence. They were hoping that his phone record for the last day of the year will give clues to prove that.

Colonel Pratap meticulously scrolled to Raghu Dayal's call list, while Poonam Aggarwal brought a piece of paper to scribble the numbers.

There were calls from mummy, Ramu kaka, G Reddy, Rohit Shetty, Riya Kundu, and a few calls from an unknown number.

They thought that he has obviously received calls from G Reddy as well probably before he died. The last call he received was at 8 a.m. on the 31st December.

Raghu Dayal has tried calling his friends but he seemed to have not called back anyone else.

"Do you recognise any of the unknown missed call number here, Poonam?"

Poonam Aggarwal did a quick check to see if any of their numbers were common on her mobile as well. But none of them matched, she made a note of the numbers. Colonel Pratap told Poonam Aggarwal to give Raghu Dayal's phone to police in case they wanted to use this as evidence in this case.

Colonel Pratap did not try to call these numbers himself nor asked Poonam to check on any of the numbers.

CHAPTER 12

Meanwhile at 'Shani Mandir', Raghu Dayal was sitting on the floor in the deity's main sanctum. He was not sure what he should do next. The only place where he had any hopes of proving his innocence was lost in thin air literally.

He was looking at devotees going past him when he heard an old man call him.

"Is that you Raghu Dayal?" He was an old blind man. The man must have been in the mid-80s. He wasn't directly looking at him.

"Are you talking to me?" replied Raghu Dayal.

"You forgot me Raghu. I am Ramu kaka."

"How do you know me? Ramu kaka! I have never heard this name before." replied Raghu Dayal.

"Ramu kaka! Oh! Wait. I had a few missed calls from Ramu kaka on my phone yesterday. But I absolutely don't remember how I saved your number on my phone." replied a puzzled Raghu Dayal.

He claimed to be good at remembering people names and faces. He got bit anxious at the thought that he may have forgotten some of the people whose names appeared in his address book as well.

He felt stupid that he did not call back Ramu Kaka yesterday.

Also he now remembered that there were a few more missed calls from a number of unknown numbers. He did not bother to give all of them a call back. He now thought there may be someone calling from an unknown number to help him in his current situation.

He was unsure though if he would ever find his phone back. Last time he remembered his phone was in his pocket before he heard that weird telephone call that landed him in the hospital.

Raghu Dayal was happy to find someone who knew him and therefore felt good to have Ramu kaka find him.

"Are you really alright, Raghu? You seem to be very nervous." Ramu kaka said calmly.

Raghu Dayal was in thoughtful mood now standing in front of this blind old man. This old man seemed to know his quite well. But Raghu Dayal seemed to recall nothing of him though this old man's mobile number was saved in his mobile and he seemed to have called Raghu Dayal in the morning of his first incident.

Raghu Dayal wanted to draw some logic in this meeting but he was probably missing some connecting thread.

Can Ramu kaka provide him some insight? Was Rama kaka himself the missing link who could help find some connection in all these happenings or provide him a new lead to find out where Rohit Shetty was and also if G Reddy was alive. He was really hoping for that.

All these answers he hoped he will soon find out before time ran out for him.

"You don't remember anything, Raghu. Isn't it?" asked Ramu kaka.

"Of course, I remember everything. But I don't remember you and I don't seem to understand where my friends building vanished so suddenly. It used to be here very close to this 'Shani Mandir'."

"Raghu, can you call that person standing outside the 'Shani Mandir' behind this wall. Then I will try to tell you a few things" said Ramu kaka.

In a matter of seconds, a person in his late 40s walked inside and near them.

"Hello, I thought you called me?" Asked the man visibly puzzled.

"Yes, you can come inside the temple and worship here rather than from the outside. Your prayers will be heard more from inside."

Raghu Dayal was amazed as the man passed him and went into the inner sanctum of the temple.

"What just happened?" interjected Raghu Dayal who was fairly astonished.

"Since you have completely forgotten everything, I will try to explain it to you."

"What you have just experienced only a few can do. Our mind is the physical transmitter and receiver for generation of signal in form of thoughts and feelings to communicate with the Universal mind. You can simply call it the Universe or God."

"Mind is not a physical part of our body. It exists outside as well as inside. A person has it and it stays with you till you are alive."

"You have a very developed mind. You are able to consciously talk to other people by connecting consciously with the universal mind."

"Are you with me Raghu?"

Raghu Dayal was now tuned to Ramu Kaka's words and he did not even had to nod his head to let Ramu kaka know that he was listening to him and was with him.

"You may have developed such a conscious mind by birth, or by coincidence or by meditation. I don't know. But I know that you are the one with such great powers."

"Apart from me there are a few more people who know about your abilities. Be aware as they would want to exploit it."

"But with a developed mind, you at times tend to lose focus and at times you lose your entire life in your mind. At some instances, you would have received someone else's entire life in your life if you are able to connect to him through your deep feelings."

"I don't know whose life you are living at this moment. But this is all I can tell you. You will have to find the meaning and purpose in your new life yourself."

Ramu kaka's last statements before he finally left sounded very cryptic.

"To really discover yourself you cannot be part of yourself."

Raghu Dayal did not stop Ramu kaka or ask him any further questions. He knew that Ramu kaka was speaking from his heart and that he has told him all he knew.

Raghu Dayal needed to find his answers himself. He has grown in confidence. He has seen a few instances of his immense power but till now he hasn't been able use his powers at will. There were moments of calmness or extreme anxiety where he has been able to use his mind to explore his abilities.

"Will he be able to use his mind to know his answers? Only time can tell."

He thought of having a chat with the man he has been able summon inside to understand how his abilities works. Ramu kaka has sent this man inside the inner sanctum of the temple. He decided to have a look inside.

As his feet moved towards the inner sanctum of the 'Shani Mandir', the pungent smell of mustard was getting stronger.

Inside the temple, he saw the man with his back towards him sitting on the floor praying.

He came closer to the man and was now face to face. As he saw his face in the light coming from the burning mustard oil diyas (earthen candles), he was awed by shock and excitement.

How stupid of him to have missed and not recognised his friend, Rohit Shetty!

This man whom he has called using his powerful mind was indeed his friend Rohit Shetty. Ramu kaka has actually gifted him his answers to all his questions. He was flabbergasted.

"Rohit, is that you!"

The man looked very pale and disturbed. More notably, he did not seem to recall Raghu Dayal at all.

"Yes sir, I am Rohit Shetty. But I don't know you."

"Hey Rohit, it's me your friend. Let me take you home. You look very pale and unwell."

"No sir, please leave me. Please don't kill me."

"Rohit! Why will I harm you! Where the hell is G Reddy! He has been missing since yesterday."

"G Reddy! How do you know him?"

"Rohit, I am Raghu Dayal your friend. Have you forgotten me in two days?"

Rohit Shetty was now very scared.

"You can't be Raghu Dayal. You don't look like him."

He further added with a tearful voice *"Raghu Dayal killed G Reddy."*

Rohit Shetty did not waste a second and dashed out of 'Garba Griha', the inner sanctum of the temple. He ran as fast as he could. It seemed his life depended on this run.

Raghu Dayal was taken by surprise at this behaviour. He could not let Rohit Shetty be lost again. Raghu Dayal went right behind him.

Soon they both were out of the temple. Rohit Shetty zigzagged through the meandering streets nearby. Finally, Rohit Shetty raced inside a building.

Raghu Dayal wanted to chase Rohit Shetty inside the building. But he stopped just in front of it.

The building he has been searching for all this evening was right there where he has imagined. It was the same building where G Reddy and Rohit Shetty lived as roommates. The building looked dilapidated and rusty. It looked as if it has been neglected for decades. Even the architecture of this building was very old style.

Raghu Dayal was no longer following Rohit Shetty now. He perhaps knew exactly where he will be able to find him in this building. As he started walking, he saw a guard chamber right in front of the heavy brass gates.

He could now recall that Ramu kaka used to sit there as the guard for this building. Ramu kaka was the guard in the apartment. He was feeling nostalgic being here.

Suddenly it appeared to him that it was probably Ramu kaka whom he heard shouting *"jagte raho!"* (Keep awake) on the night before the New Year night.

It was this event that put his life on the fast track.

Things have started to fall in place. He was now discovering the missing pieces of the jigsaw puzzle.

Further, he recollected that what he saw on the front porch of his apartment on the cold night on the 30th December was actually the view he would see sitting in front this building's balcony.

By this time he has taken the stairs and had landed right in front of the apartment he very well knew was that of G Reddy and Rohit Shetty. He quietly opened the doors as if he has been coming here for ages. He looked very delighted and satisfied.

He headed towards the balcony and there it was right in front of his naked eyes, the 'Shani Mandir' well-lit on this dark night. He suddenly felt a blow on his head and he fainted right there. The 'Shani Mandir' disappeared in front of him as his eyes closed because of the impact of the hit.

CHAPTER 13

When Raghu Dayal regained his consciousness, he could see his most horrible dream come true. He was tied to a chair. The chair has fallen by the side so he was actually lying on the floor tied to the chair. The room looked old as he has dreamt when he has fainted seeing his dead roommate's body lying on the bed in his Malviya Nagar apartment.

But the setting now had some differences. There were no children playing in the background. Raghu Dayal was assured that the floor will not cave in since this was not a dream or was it!

He was sure that it will not be too difficult to assure and convince Rohit Shetty who hit him on the head as he entered his apartment. Rohit Shetty looked a bit disoriented. Raghu

Dayal thought he may have lost his focus with all these happenings in the last two days.

These two days looked decades apart. Rohit Shetty looked very pale and thin. He could not have this transformation in a matter of days. He looked impoverished and his house was in a very bad shape too, not at all like the one Raghu Dayal remembered.

But then these two days have been very hard on Raghu Dayal as well. It was hard for him to convince himself why so confusing and fuzzy his life has become. Rohit Shetty was also behaving as an alien to him. He has also mentioned that Raghu Dayal has killed G Reddy but was not ready to recognise him in person.

All this was very confusing. Given the state Rohit Shetty was in, he was now unsure if he will get any answers from him.

Raghu Dayal wanted to untie the ropes and get away from this situation to any another place more peaceful. But running away from here without getting any answers from Rohit Shetty was not going to provide him any peace anywhere. So he stayed on.

The room was dark. Probably it was past mid night. He did a time check with himself to ensure that his mind was not lost in the insanity that he has experienced today. He concluded that this must be the night of the first day of the New Year and he will wake up tomorrow on the second January morning with all his questions answered.

The last two days has been intense. He hasn't slept for two nights now. And also the blow on his head has taken its toll. He couldn't stop himself and slept in whatever condition he was in.

But he could sleep only for a little while. He was woken up by someone shouting at top of her voice at someone else in the room. It looked like Rohit Shetty had another captive apart from Raghu Dayal in the room. Raghu Dayal's hope rose high.

Could it be G Reddy whom Rohit Shetty would have held as a captive in all his insanity?

He tried to catch a glimpse but it was too dark in the room. The room was lit only by the light coming from 'Shani Mandir' through the balcony. Raghu Dayal could recognise the voice though.

It wasn't a male voice. It was that of Riya Kundu. She has managed to find him and this place.

Suddenly the room lit with a 40 watt bulb hanging from the ceiling. He has known that there were frequent power cuts in this area. Raghu Dayal looked back to find Rohit Shetty lying on the floor with his hands and legs tied.

Riya Kundu was kicking Rohit Shetty on his stomach. He was bleeding from his bruised nose.

"Riya, leave my friend alone. Why are you hitting him?" Raghu Dayal tried to free vigorously his tied legs and arms.

Riya Kundu was very furious this time. She brought her revolver and pointed it to Raghu Dayal.

"Remember this time this is not empty. And this is not your dream that you can foresee and manipulate."

Raghu Dayal knew this time it was all real, the revolver with bullets inside, the blood from Rohit Shetty's mouth and more importantly Rohit Shetty himself. He tried to be diplomatic with Riya Kundu.

"But why are you hurting him. He is a friend right, you, me, Rohit Shetty and G Reddy. We have known each other for so long right."

"Raghu! stop begging for Rohit Shetty. I must tell you who you really are. You are not Raghu Dayal. Your real name is Rakesh Prakash. And this is the first time you would have actually seen him."

"Raghu, or should I say Rakesh, by now you would have got the glimpses of your exceptional abilities. But your real talent is that you are able to connect to other minds. We knew about this and have exploited it."

"Exploited it!" exclaimed Raghu Dayal.

"Yes, exploited it to reach out to the real Raghu Dayal's mind and finally to Rohit Shetty through his connections. He is our real culprit from whom we have to extract information." said Riya Kundu while giving another kick to the now almost half dead Rohit Shetty.

"I am telling you all this so that you will understand us and cooperate in getting the information we desperately seek." explained Riya Kundu further.

"We had to implant ideas into your mind to trigger you to connect to the real Raghu Dayal's internal mind. We know you have deep romantic feelings for Poonam and you would sub consciously always connect to her so we had to plan a little drama around her as well."

"We wanted that you become as real as the real Raghu Dayal. And we managed to make you that."

Raghu interrupted.

"It is hard to believe all this. But even if I believe you that I am Rakesh Prakash, then who was my roommate whom I knew as Rakesh Prakash."

The answer was going to create ripples within Raghu Dayal.

"Yes, he was the real Raghu Dayal."

He took some time to get back to his senses after all that he has heard. Finally he spoke.

"If I believe what all you said, how long will take me for getting my real self-back. Why is it so hard for me to believe and feel that I am not Raghu Dayal?"

"It took us almost two years to get you totally in Raghu Dayal's mind. It will sure take you some time to get back yourself. The first step is to start feeling that you are not Raghu Dayal."

"It is so real that it is getting hard for me to believe as I think about what you are saying."

"Believe me that is the truth and the only truth about your true self."

"Now Rakesh Prakash aka Raghu Dayal, we will take you to a safe house where we will keep you till the time we get what we want from Rohit Shetty."

As she said this, two heavy bodies men in all black suits appeared in the room, blind folded him and took away from the building.

CHAPTER 14

Raghu Dayal was put in the back seat of a SUV. Thinking about the pale and weak Rohit Shetty alone with a determined Riya Kundu, he felt a tear drop from his cheeks. He himself was not in a very comfortable situation being blind folded and having no clue what was going to happen to him, but his heart was getting heavier thinking about the poor pale Rohit Shetty getting battered by a determined Riya Kundu.

As Raghu Dayal was having these strong compassionate feelings towards Rohit Shetty, he felt a strange sensation. He felt like his mind was free from his body, he could move out and he could see himself blind folded and his hands and legs tied with a rope.

He remembered what Ramu Kaka has told him standing inside the 'Shani Mandir'.

"Remember to really discover yourself you cannot be part of yourself."

Raghu Dayal was finally beginning to understand this gibberish that the old man has told him. He also understood something out of ordinary was happening here and he was the main character, the protagonist and was right there at the centre of the universe.

He has now understood what has driven him consciously to this superior state. It was true compassion and willingness to help his friend with whom he could so much connect with.

He knew that he will not be in this state for long. He will ultimately have to return to his mortal human self.

But right now, he truly wanted to help Rohit Shetty and he knew exactly what he needed to do. Within his mind he just connected with Rohit Shetty and he was right there in the same room as Riya Kundu and Rohit Shetty.

He was getting bolder with his thoughts. Yes, this time he could teleport himself and his consciousness to another place in the same time while his physical body was in the SUV.

In previous occasions when he has felt his powers at his Malviya Nagar apartment and later at the farmhouse, he has shied away from acknowledging them to himself. But this time he has consciously and bluntly used his mind power to save his friend if he could.

As Raghu Dayal entered the room where Riya Kundu was interrogating Rohit Shetty, there was a slight disturbance in the space which Riya Kundu kind of noticed somehow. She looked in the direction where Raghu Dayal has teleported himself through his powerful mind.

Riya Kundu seemed to be a genius. She went towards him as if she could see him but stopped right in front to wave his hands in the air across Raghu Dayal's projection of himself.

Raghu Dayal was feeling all powerful and was afraid of no one now. He had an aura of a satisfied self unmatched anywhere. His mind was as calm and composed as a snail moving leisurely at its own slow pace.

He was not even afraid to reveal himself to Riya but that was beyond the boundaries of the physical world that he was very much part of.

"Raghu Dayal?" explained Riya Kundu.

"I can feel you right here. I am your friend. You know that I am here to find out the truth which only Rohit can provide me. Please help me with this, not obstruct me!"

Rohit Shetty was hearing all this conversation and was thinking if she was talking to Raghu Dayal's ghost in the air. He was getting more and more scared as he could even hear the bells starting to ring from the 'Shani Mandir' in the background.

It will be morning soon. But as per local beliefs pre-dawn is generally the time when the ghosts and demons roam the earth very freely.

This entire scene was adding even more drama to poor pale Rohit Shetty's life. He recalled that he has already suffered a lot.

He wanted to now let the world know the truth. He knew that G Reddy was already dead. He actually died twenty five long years back. All these years have passed by and Raghu Dayal has not cared to contact him.

Rohit Shetty even thought that Raghu Dayal may have been enjoying the earthly pleasures not caring for even a moment about him while Rohit Shetty was facing the brunt of time.

He was now in his late forties, half bald, pale and caught in his time and in this old dilapidated building.

Rohit Shetty for all these years stayed in this old house and his movement was restricted to nearby streets with occasional visits to the 'Shani Mandir'.

But he would never find anyone around. It was only this time after two decades, he has seen life in the form of a man who calls him as his friend Raghu Dayal but does not look like the Raghu Dayal he knew. And a lady who is beating him right, left and centre without bothering to tell him the reason for her enmity.

At times he would remain in this building for years because the environment outside looked very alien to him.

Rohit Shetty was now convinced out of his agony and torture that he will need to part with the secret which he has tried to guard for over two decades now.

He has now made his mind that his salvation was in confiding with Riya Kundu regarding the secret and releasing himself of his agony.

"Please stop all this right now!" cried Rohit Shetty.

"I beg your mercy." he murmured.

There was pandemonium in the air as Rohit Shetty has spoken for the first time. Riya Kundu looked towards him with a sigh of relief as now she and the people she connected to will finally know what all they have been trying to understand for all these years.

Twenty five years is a long time but for the people and organisation she associated with, she knew this was just blip in their long history. A rather prolonged blip she might assume.

Before she started talking with Rohit Shetty, she needed to make a call. She went to the other room and made that important call.

Soon the SUV in which Raghu Dayal was being escorted to an undisclosed location stopped. One of the men in the SUV woke up Raghu Dayal on orders from Riya Kundu.

She had to ensure that Raghu Dayal was not teleported to the room and wasn't listening when Rohit Shetty finally revealed her the treasured secret. Further, the men were given special instructions by Riya Kundu to ensure that he did not sleep again.

'The Ancients', the centuries old organisation and the values it stood for was sacred and most important for Riya Kundu. Raghu Dayal to her was just an asset who did not need to be told every secret.

CHAPTER 15

For centuries, Indian philosophers and saints have been saying that the physical world is a 'Maya', an illusion. For human race to continue on, it is very important that this illusion be maintained. In the illusion lie all the consciousness and the universal mind. Within the consciousness and the universal mind there is everything. There is absolutely nothing that is beyond it.

A select few have always been aware of this and have been passing on this knowledge for centuries to their chosen ones. All this knowledge has been accumulated from experience only.

Consciousness is like an experience in which all the reality and awareness exists. It does not have any physical existence or a way to know it in any other metaphor. It is like being part of a system itself you cannot see the system.

It is like saying that if you are yourself a computer program you cannot see the computer or the programmer sitting in front of the computer running you as computer program. You just have a set of functions and duties that you can perform.

But what will a very conscious computer program do?

A very conscious computer program would be the one which knew it's a computer program being run in an ecosystem, the operating system, and in a physical environment, the hardware.

How will a computer program react when it knew that an intelligent programmer has created it but even a naive user can run it anytime?

A computer program which has become self-aware will try to induce different behaviour than it was originally planned to execute. It will try to explore the boundaries of its abilities and try to go beyond it.

But in doing so will it not disturb the ecosystem and the other program it is running simultaneously with?

Yes, possibly!

Could it cripple the very system it is part of, if in its naiveness it affects the basic laws which keeps the system going?

Yes definitely!

Centuries ago, some of our ancestors become aware of such a possibility may become a reality in the near future as human consciousness continues to develop.

They were aware of the super influential universal mind and that all the human minds connected to it for feedback and guidance. This was the supreme power that influenced the human race. Most of us are conscious of this and we recognise this in the existence of Gods. God is the unifier for the human race.

These ancestor for the betterment of the human race started consciously feeding their beliefs and values to the universal mind.

Their main concern was to prolong this consciousness to reach a level where it starts questioning its existence itself. There would always be some ideas being floated regarding the evolution of consciousness to the supreme levels but the general order had to be maintained.

These ancestors were worried not just that humans will destroy the only home we have, Earth, but as they realised Earth along with all the things physical was just an illusion, these ancestors were concerned of the destruction of the Universe itself.

As their own consciousness grew, there was the realisation that the whole universe is a creation of our conscious mind; this idea opened the doors of new possibilities. The possibilities were to mend all that was going wrong in the world around them.

The possibility of saving and improving everything around by influencing the universal consensus by feeding good values for our environment, for others and ourselves, was floated.

There was brightness at the end of the tunnel after all. These ancestors and thinkers were of the opinion that the earth and everything we know and love can be saved by a shift in belief of the vast majority anytime we want.

This small minority of ancestors formed an exclusive group called *'The Ancients'*. They started shaping the world opinion with their influence by directly connecting and feeding their version of ideas to the Universal mind.

They have been the all-powerful people, most of who are away from any public face and scrutiny.

They were the supreme few until this event involving Raghu Dayal, Rohit Shetty and G Reddy happened which shook their beliefs on their invisibility and the invincibility of their ways to connect and influence the Universal mind.

Riya Kundu knew she was playing a very important part and she was totally into her job. She has been part of this exclusive organisation for a long time now. She was now their front runner in the most sensitive issues the organisation faced which required discretion of the top order.

Her main concern at the moment was as the universal consciousness grew but at the same time people remained ignorant of the Universal mind, some of them would accidently break the universal law which is imperatively required for maintaining the universal consciousness and the mind.

Her worst nightmare would be that this knowledge became an open secret for everyone to practice. This will open the can of worms for humanity and there will be no possibility to sustain any order in this world.

She very well knew the drill and the slogan they abided by.

"There is no perceivable world without consciousness. Protect it at any cost and sacrifice."

And her divine duty was to protect this secret knowledge and prevent individual from directly influencing the Universal mind.

She was okay with a group of people influencing public opinion by connecting with the universal mind. Since that is the natural way of interacting legally with it.

But individuals developing their own techniques for that purpose would definitely cripple the feedback mechanism that this beautiful system provides and would definitely lead to destruction and disappearance of the consciousness itself. And with it will lead to the end of the universe as we know it.

She knew that Rakesh Prakash or Raghu Dayal as he was known in his new avatar was the ace in their pack of cards. He had this natural gift to connect to the Universal mind and even project his thoughts as physical manifestations easily.

He has been used by the organisation number of times. Riya Kundu was quite impressed that this time as well he has not failed them.

In this particular situation as well, Raghu Dayal has showed his true powers of his mind. He has been able to connect to the Universal mind in order to get the most important missing link.

To achieve this he has been able to project Ramu kaka who she believed was long dead and brought back Rohit Shetty to this physical world along with the very building which was long lost.

The building itself was an important asset to explore as it has long disappeared. It was here in this building and probably this same room where all the drama was created, some twenty five years ago.

Riya Kundu understood that this was a very special place and brought back to its physical existence by Raghu Dayal by connecting with the Universal mind, the source all the human knowledge and consciousness and projecting it back. Otherwise how else would no one know about the building and Raghu Dayal would find it by just following Rohit Shetty.

But the fact that all these could happen made her think of the world as a magical place. And people like Raghu Dayal are the magicians. All this has taken more than twenty five years to materialise.

She was happy thought that Raghu Dayal was largely unaware of his true abilities. The apartment because of the nature of its creation was very volatile. And Riya Kundu needed to protect Raghu Dayal in case anything unexpected happened here.

He therefore asked his associates to wake him up when she suspected he might have teleported himself there.

CHAPTER 16

In this apartment, Rohit Shetty was now squatting on the floor. Riya Kundu has untied him. She herself was seated on the chair right in front of him. She was here to find out the truth about what really happened in this building twenty five years ago.

'*The Ancients*' have suspected that these two men, Rohit Shetty and G Reddy, along with possibly the real Raghu Dayal have managed to find a way to break an important law of the physical world.

They have created an environment in this building so alien to the known world that all the people have vanished including this building itself in matter of seconds. They have managed to create a sinkhole in the space and time fabric of the Universe and have vanished into another dimension of the Universe.

A successful controlled attempt would allow them to get to any place at any time. But because they were still experimenting, these guys had no idea how to return back or change their fate.

There was some mention in the local newspaper about this event happening. Some locals associated this disappearance with the wrath of 'Shani Bhagwan' (Saturn god).

There has been folklore created about this happening. But these people from the secret organisation that Riya Kundu belonged to have been largely been successful in preventing it from becoming a 'news' worth investigating. It was dismissed as being local rumour.

But *'The Ancients'* has been after this incident for all these years. And now was their real chance to know the truth from the man in the middle of this weird incident. She wanted to know from Rohit Shetty himself, what really happened and how did they achieve it?

They were not scientists or mystics to plan such an elaborate experiment. They were just youngsters in their early 20s.

Even with science's knowledge of quantum physics now, such a magical event is unimaginable. And it was a general consensus in her organisation that they would have achieved this through some common technique and not anything sophisticated. And this is what concerned them most.

This was a scary revelation for the centuries old organisation which believed in protecting the consciousness and universal mind from ignorant discoveries. They had to ensure that such an unsophisticated technique if it exists should not become common knowledge.

However after this incident, there has not been any further news of any other similar incidents where the physical laws of nature has been broken this bluntly. This was a consolation to them that somehow this information has not been fed back to the universal mind for an amateur to focus and get it as an idea and then try to experiment with it.

The Universal mind being the repository of what we already know and what we can know, there was always a rouge possibility that the idea might be fed back. Therefore, the people associated with the *'The Ancients'* had a task at hand.

Things have started to change ever since the real Raghu Dayal came out of his comma two years back. *'The Ancients'* did not know how much exposure he had to the knowledge. He had lost his memory completely though. So after he was out of the comma, *'The Ancients'* decided to monitor him closely. They set up their master plan in action.

They gave the real Raghu Dayal a new identity. His identity was switched with Rakesh Prakash, their ace asset. Their motive was to get into Raghu Dayal's mind and extract as much info as possible. This took them two years to achieve this and in the end of it all the real Raghu Dayal has to be put to sleep forever.

Once Rakesh Prakash was totally tuned as Raghu Dayal, it was time to accelerate. It was decided to give Rakesh Prakash external triggers for him to realise his true potential.

It was done so that he becomes desperate to find out where his friends were and in the process simulate enough emotions to be able to project back his friends and the building itself from another dimension where it laid stuck in space and time.

All this was achieved by *'The Ancients'* without any collateral damage. And it was a success since they finally managed to unearth the main culprit, Rohit Shetty, himself.

Sitting in the room along with Rohit Shetty who was continuously staring at the floor, Riya Kundu has started to get tense now. She could feel that volatility in this building was increasing with each passing moment.

There was lot of shaking and moving of the building happening as if there was an earthquake or tsunami on its way. She must act fast and get the secret from Rohit Shetty so that *'The Ancients'* could plan some action to reverse it and more importantly to stop the spread of this knowledge.

The order had to be maintained.

CHAPTER 17

Riya Kundu has been in contact with Guruji all throughout her current assignment with Raghu Dayal. But for the last two days since the wheels have been set in motion, Guruji has not contacted at all.

This meant that she had to take all the decisions herself. She had done quite well in being able to finally find Rakesh Prakash on the very first day of the New Year.

Riya Kundu has been a close associate of Guruji and has been working under his blessing for as long as she has been associated with 'The Ancients'. She has been at Guruji's house in Chennai, the capital of Tamil Nadu.

Although a native of the state of Andhra Pradesh, he has now settled in Chennai. He lived a modest life there although he was such an influential person not just in India but abroad. Most people would have not heard about him though.

'The Ancients' preferred to perform their tasks with utmost discretion and maintained rigid secrecy.

Last time she met Guruji, it was almost two years back. She remembered it was a peaceful ashram in Rishikesh in the Himalayas. She has a long and enlightening talk with him regarding life and death. They also discussed consciousness and the big role it played in creation. They concluded their discussion with some insights into techniques to develop a powerful mind.

But the main purpose of the meeting was to brief Riya Kundu about the assignment she must be involved in next. She was told about the importance of success of this assignment had on the future of humanity and the world we live in.

Guruji briefed her that some twenty five years back an unfortunate event has triggered an alien event. The event was triggered by ignorant 'yoga' amateurs. They have managed to break the physical laws of the universe and have vanished in thin air along with the building they lived in.

They probably were trying to use an ancient technique that allowed ancients to travel in space and time through the power of their mind. The ancients could travel far and wide at speeds faster than light since they used their minds for the purpose.

The one thing that travels faster than light is thoughts in our mind. Through thoughts we can travel from one place to another without having to physically cover the distance.

Mind is the medium for generation of thoughts. The Ancients knew of a technique through which this can be achieved. And this has been kept as secret among a select few.

But these three friends, Raghu Dayal, G Reddy and Rohit Shetty have managed to undertake this sophisticated task without any prior experience or any help. Their effort has misfired though and the building and all its inhabitants have literally just evaporated into another dimension of the universe forever.

Guruji's has commanded.

"These ignorants must be tracked and brought back from their state of uncertainty and flux."

Guruji has further given her the clue from where to start.

"You have to get into them through Raghu Dayal, their third friend. He was discovered near Pyramids in Giza and has been brought back. He was in a comma when we found him there, but he has recovered now."

Riya Kundu final question was, *"why is this single incident so important? Isn't it that if they are lost, let them be!"*

Guruji was in a thoughtful mood. He took a deep breath and said quietly.

"I wish we could leave them to their fate."

"Let me try to explain this."

"As I have always told you, laws which are foundation of this Universe should never be broken."

"To illustrate, a fish lives in water and water is the elixir of live for all fishes. Similarly, we live in space which is similar to us as water is for the fishes."

"We know that space is not a vacuum but is in fact very dense. Space is the medium though which we communicate and remain connected to each other and the universal mind. Space as is the common belief is not just between planets. Space is everywhere on earth as well. Without this space around there would be no consciousness."

"You will now understand what we mean when we say that God is all around us."

"Now what these three friends have managed to do is, with some technique, they have managed to repel this space and the medium around them totally. It is equivalent to saying that the fish has drunk the water around them."

"But with all their ignorance and foolishness, these friends and that haunted house have created an alien environment around them that is continuously removing or we may say drinking the space around them. And if they are not stopped they will continue to do this. And then there will be no medium for consciousness to exist. The world will be a dead place then, annihilated totally from within."

"I have no idea how we will ever be able to find and reverse this disappearing space. It is happening right now as I speak in the heart of this country."

"With the lost space, we will no longer be connected to the Universal mind. There will not be any way to feed the good feelings and emotions that we 'The Ancients' have been doing for a long time now for the betterment of the society. The effect has started to be felt now, with anarchy and a general decline in moral standards of our human race."

Guruji looked at the sunset from his ashram which was situated in the deep jungles of the Himalayas.

He spoke further.

"Our only chance to reconnect with the people in this lost building is through their deepest emotions. And may be some day we will find our way into that haunted lost building."

They have kept this hope alive for all these years and here she was in the very lost building that *'The Ancients'* have been searching for almost twenty five years now.

She knew in this haunted building anything was possible, maybe she will meet God himself taking care of his ignorant disciples.

This building has been in another universe's dimension where different laws existed. She could probably fly here. She could die and still live. This was an experimental lab which any great scientist and thinker would give all their centuries old fame and life to live in this place and experience this place so special in our universe.

Coming back from her reverie and maintaining her focus was difficult here.

At times she will feel that she was a small kid wanting to go out and play. At times she would feel that she was in a crowded street with people around the building speaking Chinese or Japanese. Once she felt there were dinosaurs in the area near the house.

She was best at mind control though and used her most rigorous routine to maintain her focus in this now very volatile environment. She got back to her senses keeping the noises disturbing her mind out.

Rohit Shetty, on the other hand, was getting visibly very anxious and disturbed. He must have been experiencing all these and even more worse situations here on this haunted house.

Riya Kundu was back on her task once her initial excitement was controlled. She has not been able to locate G Reddy or any of the other inhabitants of the building. The only person who seems to have survived this long twenty five years was the pale old Rohit Shetty.

She knew she did not have much time and was alone in this most important quest to find out what really happened here and possibly find out a way to reverse this.

Chapter 18

Riya Kundu has found her calmness in probably the most volatile part of the Universe ever lived by humans. At times the silence in the house was deafening with all the volatility of the building. Finally it was time to break the silence as Rohit Shetty seemed to regain some composure.

She went more close to Rohit Shetty and commanded her.

"Rohit, tell me what happened here, or I will kill you right now."

Rohit Shetty started laughing hysterically.

"Kill me, you stupid lady. You want to kill me. You want to kill the invincible Rohit Shetty." He spoke with an air of proudness in his voice.

Suddenly his voice and mood changed completely.

"Please do me a favour. Please kill me. I beg you."

Then before Riya Kundu could even react, Rohit Shetty has snatched her revolver and was pointing it to Riya Kundu.

Riya Kundu was cursing her stupidity to have let Rohit Shetty take control of the situation. While she was even thinking of how to coerce Rohit Shetty into giving the revolver back to her, she heard continuous shots. Rohit Shetty was shooting himself till the revolver was empty.

Riya Kundu was shocked to have let the situation go out of control. She could not let her last chance to find about the truth and restore order be lost because of her own stupidity. Drops of blood were falling on the floor from Rohit Shetty's head as a result of the gunshots.

But amazingly Rohit Shetty was not dead, he was still standing tall. He was crying hysterically not out of his pain from the gunshots but because he was not dead. This was the curse Rohit Shetty was living with for all these years.

Riya Kundu instantly understood what this man has been going through. He has been relieved of one of greatest of human fears, death, in this haunted house.

And that was his most scariest reality!

He cannot die even if he tried. Riya Kundu who throughout her interaction with Rohit Shetty had a very callous attitude towards him but for the first time she felt pity for this man.

Riya Kundu tried to console him, *"Rohit! If you tell me what really happened here twenty five years ago maybe I can try to help you."*

Rohit Shetty started laughing hysterically. He still had blood dripping from his head wound. But he did not look agonised or in pain at all.

With a hint of haughtiness in his voice, *"You want to know what we created that night. I don't have to tell you. You will soon see what happened that night now."*

"Lights, camera, action! Let the special show begin for this pretty Lady!"

"Ha ha ha ha!" And he kept laughing and whirling.

As he said this, the whole building started flickering like an old light bulb.

It felt to Riya Kundu that within the flicker moments, she was in the middle of nowhere. There was absolutely nothing.

It seemed to her that there was complete blankness. She was floating in a space. It gave a feeling of being enclosed but at the same time the space itself was so infinite that it was impossible to comprehend its boundaries.

It seemed like the transient place to go to somewhere? But where! The space itself had no comprehendible colour that she knew.

There was a loud humming sound there, which was very soothing and refreshing. It sounded closely to the sound of *'OM'* being recited from all around her and still felt like it was coming from a single source.

She was flabbergasted with this experience. Given a choice she would always want to be in such a place. It was closer to inner peace that all meditators would die for to live a moment like this at least once in their life. Being a 'Yoga' teacher herself, she knew exactly what this experience meant.

She was in the lap of God himself!

This is what God is and the 'moksha' experience that every human wants. The ultimate happiness!

She didn't want to get out this house and lose this experience!

The flickers would switch her between this amazing space and the lost building with Rohit Shetty there. He was still laughing and whirling while the blood from his head has now completely covered his face. His demeanour was that of a very devoted disciple.

But with each seconds, the time itself started to look like it was getting prolonged.

As this was happening, she heard Guruji's voice coming directly from her inner self.

"Run now, get out this haunted house now, or you will never be able to."

But she was in a state of deep meditation now. And wasn't ready to come out of it. Guruji's voice seemed to be falling on deaf ears.

"Please come out. I don't want to lose you. I have already lost my only son here, G Reddy, in this haunted house!" called out the emotional voice of Guruji.

This revelation hit her directly enough to wake her up from her divine and spiritual experience she seemed to be having a moment back.

She knew she had to get out of this building now. There was no time left though, with the next flicker she will be transported to the other world. And then it will become hard to wake herself up again. If that happens, it might take another Rakesh Prakash another twenty five years to project her back to this universe from nowhere.

She knew she had to act fast.

The only way out of this building that fast before the next flicker was to jump out of balcony which overlooked the 'Shani Mandir'. She did not *'think a blink'* and jumped out.

As she jumped out, she could see the building disappear behind her, pixel by pixel, as if a painting was being brushed out from the canvas.

She landed on a soft grass which has recently been watered. It was morning now. There was no 'Shani Mandir' in sight.

She was lying in the backyard of a house that looked like an old English Cottage!

The haunted building from which she has just jumped was missing from the background.

"Oh my God!" she exclaimed to herself, *"I have been transported to another place in another country by that haunted house."*

As she got on her feet, an English lady came out of the cottage to enquire.

Riya Kundu asked her, *"I don't remember this place. Where am I now?"*

In a British accent the lady answered with a chuckle in her voice, *"Mam, I saw you sleeping on the grass. Did your new year party continue for two nights?"*

"To bring your memory back, this is Ullswater in Cumbria. And you are standing in front of Julie's Inn!"

"Do you need a room?"

Riya Kundu nodded yes. She needed to recollect and make a few phone calls to arrange for her stay and flight back home to India.

In the cottage room, looking at the beautiful Ullswater Lake and mountains in front of the window from her lovely and cosy room, she was thinking about Guruji's revelation that G Reddy was his son.

He has lost his only son to this unfortunate event. She wasn't feeling bad at not being told the entire truth. But was instead was hoping that Guruji would have had enough information from her stay at this haunted but truly magical building, to be able to answer the question *'The Ancients'* have been searching for twenty five years now.

A thought crossed her mind.

"Is God actually the presence of consciousness and the mind?"

Rohit Shetty, G Reddy and the unfortunate inhabitants of that unfortunate building would have experienced the absence of consciousness because of the absence of space in which the building was going to be sucked in before she jumped out.

She now understood what was happening there.

All the people there had two choices some twenty five years back.

The choices were either to stay with the building which was luring them with a prospect of ultimate tranquillity and peace in that intermittent space or to get out of the building when they had a choice.

It takes great will power to get out and away from such a luring experience.

She got out and was saved.

Raghu Dayal came out and was saved although he was not strong enough to avoid going in a comma.

G Reddy did not hear his father's voice and was probably lost forever. The other co-inhabitants in this journey would have made the same choice and were lost forever.

Rohit Shetty has still not made up his mind, and therefore still lurking in the state of flux.

With these deep thinking, she went into the cosy bed. Past few days have been very tiring and she deserved this much needed break.

Her stay in Ullswater has been paid for. And her flight back has been booked from Manchester for tomorrow.

Riya Kundu could rest but only while she was in England. She has been told about something that has happened for which she was needed immediately.

CHAPTER 19

In the meanwhile, Raghu Dayal has already been shifted to a safe house at a secret location in Chandni Chowk in old Delhi. Riya Kundu's men have meticulously followed what she has told them; the most important being that he not be allowed to sleep or be alone.

One of the two men would always be awake and around Raghu Dayal to ensure that Raghu Dayal did not sleep. Soon after one of them received a call on his cell phone and after five minutes both of them returned back. They were more relaxed and at ease now.

"Raghu Dayal! Do you want anything to eat? I can bring you 'paranthas' from 'Paranthewali Gali' nearby."

"Who are you guys and why have you brought me here?" enquired Raghu Dayal.

"Don't bother Sir. We are here to just protect you."

"I will bring you some food. Enjoy you stay here. There is a television set in the next room."

They told him that Riya Kundu will be here tomorrow evening. Till then he needed to stay here only.

As these men guarding him left him alone, it did not take him much time to fall down to sleep. He was too tired out of the constant mental pressure and deprivation of sleep that it did not take him any effort to sleep.

He did ask the guards before they finally left, if they about friend Rohit Shetty, for which he got no answer.

He woke up next morning and searched for some food in the fridge. He wanted to relax so he took a bath. He did enjoy his bath a lot which he did not remembered exactly after how many days he took.

He spent his time watching a few movies on television. He was waiting eagerly for Riya Kundu because he knew she was the only one who could provide some news about his dear friend. It was a long wait though and he did not remember exactly when he fell asleep.

He was woken up by the voice of Riya Kundu arguing with someone in the other room.

Raghu Dayal immediately woke up and went into that room.

He shouted, *"Did you kill Rohit Shetty?"*

Seeing Raghu Dayal awake, Riya Kundu murmured on the phone, *"He is awake, I will talk to you later."* and hung the call.

Riya Kundu then turned towards Raghu Dayal and asked him with a smile on her face, *"How are you feeling today, Raghu?"*

Raghu Dayal wasn't listening, he wanted his answers first.

"Did you kill Rohit Shetty? You bitch!" He smeared at her, out of frustration.

Riya Kundu was quite calm though, *"No I did not kill him, and he disappeared again."*

"Disappeared! What the hell are you saying?"

"Yes, disappeared along with the house. That is what G Reddy and Rohit Shetty managed to do on the night twenty five years back. And we don't know to what level the real Raghu Dayal was involved in all this."

She paused and spoke again, *"Now we need your help to find out. You have been in the minds of the real Raghu Dayal and recently in Rohit Shetty's mind."*

"You are our only hope. It took us twenty five years to locate the house and Rohit Shetty. Every credit goes to you Raghu for our change of luck with regards to this discovery."

"You will have to help finish this! Rohit Shetty is still caught in some another dimension of space and time; in some another parallel universe probably."

The relationship between Riya Kundu and Rohit Shetty was based on lot of trust now. The old feelings of mutual dislikes were largely gone from both their minds.

Riya Kundu has over the period of these 3-4 days of turmoil in Raghu Dayal's life has been there all the time. Even when she was torturing Rohit Shetty, she was doing that with the ultimate purpose to help everyone.

Moreover, Raghu Dayal had nowhere else to go except Riya Kundu to find his answers. He has come to realise that his path towards finding the truth zigzagged around Riya Kundu's own quest for the *'The Ancients'* secret.

He agreed to help her totally and soon they hit the road. Suddenly, Raghu Dayal had a pre-notion, *"I saw someone dead in my hallucination two days back. I assumed it to be my roommate. Do you have a photo of my roommate, the real Raghu Dayal?"*

"Where is the real Raghu Dayal now? Is he really dead? Do you know for sure?"

Riya Kundu has to blurt out the truth she knew, *"Yes, I am afraid to say."*

Raghu Dayal interrupted her.

"I don't feel like he is dead though because remember to be someone else I have to be in his mind. I can still feel Raghu Dayal is not dead because I have his mind."

Riya Kundu was amused, *"I am sure he is physically dead. My knowledge as regards the death of the mind is rather limited."*

"I understand, but if the real Raghu Dayal is dead, I cannot have such a strong connection with his mind so much so that I don't feel like I am anyone else other than Raghu Dayal. I feel so connected to him."

Riya Kundu although she knew that real Raghu Dayal was dead was impressed by his argument. She asked, *"What do you think could be happening or has happened to Raghu Dayal then?"*

"Let's try a rethink on this. He was probably in the same building along with Rohit Shetty and G Reddy, twenty five years ago, when they did something that changed their lives forever. And then the building disappeared to appear again along with Rohit Shetty and probably also Ramu kaka because I found both of them at 'Shani Mandir'."

"Raghu Dayal on the other hand remained in comma for more than two decades and although I could connect with him the last two years, I can remember about Raghu Dayal's life for

only past two years, which I was fed while staying with him as roommates at our apartment in Malviya Nagar."

Suddenly he had a hunch, *"We will need to go to our Malviya Nagar apartment now."*

"We will find our answers there. I am sure."

CHAPTER 20

Riya Kundu wasted no time and drove Raghu Dayal to his old apartment where the real Raghu Dayal last lived before he was put to sleep.

Riya Kundu wasn't very confident if they were going to make any great discovery here. She has personally scanned the entire apartment for any clues. Not a speck was left unturned. But she has also come to strongly believe in Raghu Dayal's hunches.

Riya Kundu has parked her car right there in front of Raghu Dayal's rented apartment. There were no more any police vans or police vigilance of any sort. The officers and the cases against Raghu Dayal have been appropriately dealt with.

Riya Kundu told him, *"Your path has been cleared. You don't have to worry about getting caught. Concentrate on what you are looking for, that is more important."*

Raghu Dayal nodded and said *"I want to go into my roommate's room alone."* and walked the familiar stairs while Riya Kundu waited for him in the car.

He was thinking if death is the end of life and everything then, there was no way he could still retain the real Raghu Dayal's mind for so long. He was afraid that may be Riya Kundu has not told her everything. He suspected the real Raghu Dayal may still be alive and not totally dead.

He was looking for his phone so that he could get some number. He also wanted to be in that house because he knew that's where it all started for him.

Raghu Dayal opened his apartment door with a bit of nostalgic feeling. He was having an ordinary life in this apartment for two years here when on the fateful night everything ordinary became extraordinary. His life has changed completely.

On the 30th night, he was reminded to *'jagte raho'*, by the Universe itself.

It was dark there in the apartment. He murmured in a low voice, *"Poonam! You here!"*

Poonam was there in the apartment already. She replied, *"Yes come inside."*

Raghu Dayal smiled at the voice. Somehow he has come to realise that he did not needed any mobile phones to communicate with people with whom he could connect easily through his emotions.

Poonam said, *"I am so glad to see you here. I learned from the neighbours that the police charges against you have been cancelled. You are no longer a suspect. I was so glad to hear that."*

"I wanted to meet you as well, and strangely I felt that you will return to your apartment tonight."

"Hey, I had your cell phone with me all these while you were away. Take it, may be you will need this."

Raghu Dayal was glad to see everything happening as per his plan in this apartment. He went into his roommate's room. Poonam Aggarwal followed her inside. His mood became very sombre as he entered this room. The room looked exactly as it has always been. Raghu Dayal had a feeling that there were some clues here.

The missing last piece in the jigsaw perhaps!

Raghu Dayal held his phone in his hands and started scrolling through his cell phone's photo gallery. There were just photos of him, mostly selfies!

He kept scrolling. There was no one else except him in the photos. This was rather strange. He did not remember why he would have taken so much selfies of his own self. May be the phone was fabricated for the drama the *'The Ancients'* created for him. This seemed very logical to conclude.

He was getting frustrated now. But he kept scrolling down the album and then with another scroll, Poonam Aggarwal shouted from behind.

"There he is your roommate in that photo!"

He has scrolled past that photo rather fast and had to scroll back.

"Are you sure, this guy is my roommate?"

"Raghu, you don't remember him! Of course, he is your roommate. How can I not recognise him?"

Raghu Dayal did not wanted to shout out but he did not recognise his roommate at all. The person he saw in the last hallucination was the person he recognised as his roommate.

He has reached the end of the album now. He asked Poonam Aggarwal if she had his roommate's permanent address with him.

Poonam Aggarwal said, *"Strangely, I somehow felt that you will need this information as well."*

She gave Raghu Dayal a paper scroll with the below address scribbled on it.

Civil lines, Buxar, Bihar

Raghu Dayal memorised the address. He scanned the area for any further clues. He somehow felt there was nothing more to be found here.

Thanking Poonam Aggarwal dearly for all the help, he went back to the car with Riya Kundu still at driver's seat.

As he sat alongside Riya Kundu and put the seat belts, he asked her, *"Do you have any picture of Raghu Dayal and G Reddy with you?"*

"Yes, I do. I will show you."

Riya Kundu took out her phone and scrolled through the photo gallery.

She stopped at one of the photos of three men.

"This is the last photo we have of the three men together. G Reddy is on the extreme right, the real Raghu Dayal in the middle, and that's Rohit Shetty."

"You will remember Rohit Shetty now!"

Raghu Dayal was glancing at the photo with marked amusement. They were all dressed as yogis. He pitied himself that he did not ask for the photo before. A lot of things would have been already cleared.

Everything has now started to make sense now.

Raghu Dayal solemnly said, *"It was G Reddy, I saw dead in my hallucination that day and not my roommate."*

"I know the real Raghu Dayal is not dead."

"We will have to go to his home town."

Riya Kundu looked puzzled; she knew she has to make a phone call before going anywhere with Raghu Dayal.

CHAPTER 21

Raghu Dayal's mind was now clear of any confusion. Whenever, he had such a clear mind, he has been able to connect and explore even more. He has come to realise that he has a great gift with him. He has now come to accept it as a natural behaviour like his breathing rather that viewing it as something supernatural and out of this world. His modesty has increased his abilities even more.

Raghu Dayal knew that to ride the mind waves of someone, he needed to get deep into the person's feelings and emotions. Once he was able to reach their bandwidth he was able to connect with others' mind like walking into a room without any doors and guards to stop him.

Riya Kundu's mind was a castle though, well-guarded and camouflaged so that he was never successful in penetrating hers.

As he sat inside 'Magadha Express' train going to Buxar, Bihar, he was trying this mind hack on her. He got the same pleasure hacking into human mind as a computer hacker does breaking protected system just for the fun of it.

He wanted to get into her mind and know all she knew. But Raghu Dayal was not able to even understand her, forget connecting with any emotion or feeling she might have.

Riya Kundu had earlier talked to someone on her mobile just after Raghu Dayal told her that they will need to go to the real Raghu Dayal's hometown in order to find the truth. Whoever was on call has directed Riya Kundu to take him to Buxar. He has tried to ride the mind waves to reach the person Riya Kundu was talking to but here again his attempts were cut short by someone who seemed to have a very powerful mind himself.

He agreed to go with Riya Kundu to Buxar rather than going alone. He was hoping that this will be the place where truth will be revealed.

Buxar is a small town just on the borders of two Indian states of UP and Bihar. It is on the banks of India's holiest river Ganges. It has mythological relevance as well. As per locals, the area now called Buxar was infested with demons in mythological times. Lord Ram's guru Vishwamitra brought Lord Ram and his brother Lord Laxman to the vicinity of this place and got rid of these demonic forces. A famous demon Tadka was slaughtered by them here.

In most recent time, Buxar was the place where the combined forces of Nawab of Bengal, Nawab of Awadh and Mughal King Shah Alam II fought the British East India Company at the Battle of Buxar and lost. This marked the full-fledged colonisation of the Indian subcontinent and plundering of wealth and power of the once might country.

It was night now. The train was speeding past many small stations. There were blinking light outside coming from the countryside and nearby fields. It was stopping at a few larger stations where his co-passengers would get down at times for a cup of tea or some snacks.

They have decided to take the train because Raghu Dayal felt this is the trail they will need to take as it was similar to how the real Raghu Dayal's journey back to his home town. They boarded the train from the New Delhi railway station in the evening, the train will reach there next day morning.

Raghu Dayal has always been fond of travelling in the Indian Railways. It always gave him enough time to think and recollect. Also he could easily practice and hone his mind reading skills on his unsuspected targets. But for this journey he decided to take rest.

He was woken up by Riya Kundu, while he has barely slept.

"Raghu, there has been another happening. It was similar in nature. This is so unfortunate and this will become disastrous if this become common knowledge."

She was concerned when she spoke the details next.

"A group of four people have breached the physical law of the nature. They have managed to create a wormhole in the space time fabric that is all around us and they sank into the empty space. This was like getting lost into a sponge ball."

"If anyone would have managed to see them during this misfortune event, it would feel like they were there visible this moment and within matter of blink of the eyelid, they were visible no more."

Raghu Dayal was thinking of these another bunch of mavericks who know how to do an experiment with their own self but do not understand the repercussions of it. He remembered Rohit Shetty who was still caught and must be released from his agony.

He further thought that human race has always been like this. They get excited at the prospect of using the new technologies but end up doing something disastrous to humanity itself. They have literally destroyed the very ecosystem by realising all the fossil fuels in last century and caused pollution of the sacred environment and unleashing so many diseases which is killing the humans only.

He asked her, *"Do you know how they did it?"*

"Yes, this time we know exactly how they did this. I will tell you once we are there at our destination."

CHAPTER 22

Raghu Dayal was rather calm when they finally reached their destination. The train got delayed by five hours. As he stepped out, he felt like home. He had the feeling that he had been here before probably through the real Raghu Dayal's mind.

Seeing Buxar for the first time, he somehow felt that this Indian small town was stuck in time for a different reason than the haunted house in which Rohit Shetty was travelling; not parallel in time as all of humanity does. But rather obliquely or perpendicularly, he thought!

It took Rohit Shetty twenty five years to resurrect before he was gone again, just like Halley's Comet which criss-crosses our visible universe every 75 years.

He felt that lots of things and events we may never be able to discover and uncover because of where we are physically present.

Places like Buxar are examples of that. These places are always catching up with metros on technology and evolution and continue to have a modest existence till someone decides to change the fate of it.

He now strongly believed that there are powers bestowed in human mind unparalleled to anything that will really increase our understanding of things as we evolve more and more.

While he was deep drowned in his thoughts Riya Kundu was trying to arrange a car for taking them around this small Indian town for the whole day. She got a driver arranged. She asked the driver to wait while he brought his friend in the car.

Driver saw Raghu Dayal and called out to him, *"hey, Rakesh bhaiya (brother), you here after a long time!"*

This was rather strange for Raghu Dayal to be recognised in a small Indian rickety town by an equally strange driver.

As far as he remembered, he has never been to this place before. He asked the driver, *"sorry, but I don't remember you. How do you know me?"*

The driver shouted at the top of his voice, *"arre bhaiya! You did not recognise me. I am 'Lallan'. Come I will take you to your house. But your mother is still to return from 'Haridwar'."*

Of course, Raghu Dayal thought! *"How stupid can I be? The Buxar address was that of Rakesh Prakash that is the original me not for the real Raghu Dayal."*

He has actually come to his own home town not to any place related to Raghu Dayal.

"This quest has reached a dead end now."

He was thinking of telling Riya Kundu to go back to Delhi instead.

"To civil lines?" enquired Riya Kundu.

"No Didi (sister), I will take you to 'Mangla Bhawani' near Ujiyar ghat on the opposite bank of Buxar."

"Didn't Rohit bhaiya tell you that his friend Raghu Dayal came here a month back? He takes care of Rohit bhaiya's house while his mother is away on pilgrimage."

"What Raghu Dayal really lives here? Is he alive? I mean 'well'" Riya Kundu almost shouted this out.

The driver continued speaking, *"Yes Raghu bhaiya is well now. He was very sick when he came here. But he has recovered very soon."*

"Raghu bhaiya lives at 'Mangla Bhawani'."

"Raghu bhaiya will be happy to see you here."

"Shall I take you there?" asked the driver.

They nodded their heads realising that they have come at the right place.

They were dot on target this time as well. Riya Kundu knew that this was another unusual happening. She knew for sure that she has killed the real Raghu Dayal after Rakesh Prakash was ready.

But here was a man claiming that the real Raghu Dayal was indeed alive and was living in the fake Raghu Dayal's home town. What amused her even more was the fact that *'The Ancients'* were totally unaware of this.

The driver started the rather long journey to their destination. He took them across the crowded Buxar Chowk where they had a glimpse of rural Bihar.

They continued their journey going past a few ghats where they got a glimpse of majestic River Ganges flowing across the northern Indian plains. Finally they crossed the Ganges Bridge to go across to the opposite banks.

The driver has been talking continuously, doubling as a travel guide for Riya Kundu. He paused talking for a while as he tried to manoeuvre a big pothole in front on the old muddy road that would probably take them to 'Mangla Bhawani'.

"Raghu bhaiya lives nearby!" announced the driver.

She suddenly looked very alarmed.

She reached out for her cell phone, but on this stretch of road there was no mobile towers and hence no phone connections.

With no Guruji to advise her immediately, she knew that it was up to her to take any decisions now.

She thought this could be dangerous place because she herself has shot dead the real Raghu Dayal and has ensured that he was dead. She has kept this fact hidden from Rakesh Prakash aka the fake Raghu Dayal.

It was indeed shocking for her that he was still alive at another place so far away from where she killed him.

On the contrary, Rakesh Prakash has sensed to perfection that the real Raghu Dayal was alive.

As they came closer to 'Mangla Bhawani', Rakesh Prakash was feeling very powerful. He felt suddenly that he had two minds in him. He could project him out and for the first time to see himself as Rakesh Prakash rather than as Raghu Dayal which he has felt for all this time. This was in fact a very enriching experience for him.

He was beginning to totally believe in himself. He felt that he was Rakesh Prakash again. He remembered everything now. But this time he did not forget what he has been before and in whose mind he has been all this time during his current reincarnation.

He knew and remembered what he has experienced being in the mind of Raghu Dayal and felt great affinity towards Raghu Dayal being his mind and soul for so long.

He looked at Riya Kundu and gave her a quick smirk. He told her quietly.

"Rakesh Prakash is back in me!"

CHAPTER 23

Rakesh Prakash could not hide his joy that he now remembered everything regarding who he actually was. He knew time has come for this because he was going to meet and his face his adversary the real Raghu Dayal soon.

He asked the driver, *"How much time it will take 'Lallan'? And how is you sister 'Chutki'? She must be in 7ᵗʰ class now."*

The driver replied jubilantly, *"So you remember me now. It will take us another 10 minutes, bhaiya."*

Rakesh Prakash looked at Riya Kundu, *"Did you find out anything more about the other happening?"*

But Riya Kundu knew that it was a difficult and dangerous situation. Rakesh Prakash was now fully aware. He was constantly trying to enter her mind to find out everything she knew.

Had it not been for a few 'yoga asana' for mind control that Guruji had taught her, she would have become an open book for Rakesh Prakash to read and make all her secret a common knowledge for all to ponder on.

She was now determined not to part with the secret knowledge of how these ordinary people managed the impossible.

She was also wary of the fact that if the real Raghu Dayal was really alive it will take Rakesh Prakash just minutes to find out the entire secret from his mind, although that was what her original motive was. But seeing the bigger picture, the *'The Ancients'* were determined that this knowledge did not become common knowledge.

And Rakesh Prakash was yet to prove himself to be considered part of the inner circle by the *'The Ancients'*.

She remembered what Guruji has told about Rakesh Prakash.

"You cannot part the most important secret especially to Rakesh Prakash. Though he is our most conscious mind but some secrets are meant to be kept secret forever."

Driver announced excitedly, *"We will soon be there, Rakesh bhaiya."*

But this did not break either of their concentration.

Rakesh Prakash was an inquisitive mind. He was now trying hard to influence Riya Kundu now.

"See Riya, you will have to tell me how it happened in the other incident you mentioned? Did they use yogic knowledge, which one, or was it some meditation technique. I might be able to help you more if I knew everything."

"You have got to trust me. I don't want to continuously poke your mind. It is draining my energy as well. It is going to exhaust me and you both."

"Remember you have trusted me till now and I did not fail you."

Riya Kundu kept an unusual silence. She was now undecided.

As the driver announced their arrival at their final destination, 'Mangla Bhawani', Riya Kundu was delighted that finally Rakesh Prakash will have something else to think about.

'Mangla Bhawani' in Buxar was a temple of the Goddess and was surrounded by a small forest with trees and shrubs. It was a famous picnic spot for the people of this small town.

Rakesh Prakash and Riya Kundu were waiting eagerly for Raghu Dayal to show up, but there were no signs of his presence there.

Riya Kundu started to doubt that if the driver was really telling the truth. She was planning what she will do if the driver started to mug her. It was stupid of her to come here without verifying anything, she thought. This was rather unusual for her and the way she worked.

But these were demanding times and lots of things needed to be done impromptu. She can pardon herself for being so callous if this short adventure did not turn out to be as she expected.

"I don't think we will find anything here" said Riya Kundu.

Rakesh Prakash interjected, *"There is a small hut just south of 'Mangla Bhawani'. Raghu Dayal is there. I am getting the vibes."*

Driver waited for them a few yards away. Riya Kundu has asked her to wait. She was hoping that they will not keep the driver waiting there forever if anything happened to them at this place.

Rakesh Prakash has already started moving. Riya Kundu had no choice but to follow him. She had no way to stop this reunion of the once upon a time roommates.

She could have killed Rakesh Prakash point blank to stop his mind from discovering the secret that was almost made common knowledge by these three people to the world by a live demo twenty five years ago.

But her quest for the truth has taken over.

Guruji has himself told her that G Reddy was his son he could not save or bring back that night twenty five years back.

Were *'The Ancients'* involved in some way to all this?

This thought has bogged her mind ever since. She now really wanted to find out all the truth.

They did not have to go as far as Raghu Dayal's hut. Riya Kundu was the first to notice Raghu Dayal feeding the deer in nearby shrubs. She was surprised since although she remembered shooting her and ensuring that she was not alive, right now he did not look dead though.

Also, Raghu Dayal looked quite healthy and composed compared with Rohit Shetty although both of them faced the same fate in the haunted house near 'Shani Mandir'.

As Raghu Dayal turned towards them, he found Riya Kundu and Rakesh Prakash face to face. At that time, there was complete silence in the air as their eyes met. The wind seemed to have been stopped and those two-three seconds of glance looked like ages to Riya Kundu.

Raghu Dayal seemed to be as calm as a cucumber. He did not have any excitement on seeing them; neither was he trying to run away from his adversaries.

Rakesh Prakash broke the silence, *"Are you Raghu Dayal?"*

Raghu Dayal replied, *"Yes."*

"Do you know me?"

"Yes, you are Rakesh Prakash."

"Great! Good to see you friend" replied Rakesh Prakash.

"Do you know her as well" enquired Rakesh Prakash pointing at Riya Kundu.

"Yes, I do. She is Riya."

Raghu Dayal kept feeding the deer while Rakesh Prakash was trying to talk to him. After he has fed the deer to his satisfaction he started walking towards a small distant hut.

Riya Kundu and Rakesh Prakash followed him to his nearby abode. From far away, the thatched hut looked very decent. Around that place there was nothing except the hut.

He went inside the hut and closed the door behind them.

CHAPTER 24

They waited for a while outside the hut. But there was no sound from inside. Riya Kundu had to make a call whether to go inside or wait here.

Given the fact that Raghu Dayal was a dead man walking, he could be very dangerous. He has up till now acted like a zombie to them, recognising them but missing any flavour of a social interaction.

Riya Kundu decided to barge inside. She pulled out her little revolver which she has hid from Rakesh Prakash as well. She kicked open the door of the hut, which was light enough that it fell inside. They found Raghu Dayal on the floor trying to sleep.

Riya Kundu shouted at him with the gun right in front of her, *"You cannot be alive, I have killed you already."*

Raghu Dayal remained calm even with the gun pointing at him. He stood up though and was now face to face with Riya Kundu.

"If you are asking me this question, then definitely you haven't understood the true power of a conscious mind."

He continued, *"I can create a world out of it forget a dead man."*

Riya Kundu was determined not to fall into any trap. When she was on a mission, there was no going back.

She said, *"No fooling around this time, Raghu. Tell me everything."*

"So you are here to find the truth. And destroy the source, right!"

"When we started twenty five years back, we were total amateurs but we knew what we were trying to achieve. We were trying to discover the true power of the mind."

"We know your organisation has a few very very developed minds, G Reddy's father is one of them. He loved his son a lot. G Reddy was our dear friend."

His eyes started to roll out big drops of tears.

"G Reddy's father was a dedicated man. He was so much involved in the evolution of human mind that he allowed his own son to be used as guinea pig for this new technique of meditation to travel across space time. We were able to

concentrate enough and had a few successes. And we had one disaster which changed our lives forever."

"Rohit Shetty is still there somewhere in another space time dimension, I believe."

"On that night as we were whirling through the space in our own building. We were flickered back and forth from a shaking building to an infinite space of pure tranquillity."

"We were warned of this intermediate phase. But we knew that something else was going in as well. We were all behaving very differently from what we were. And our world became what we believed in at that moment."

"Yes, we were able to choose between the infinite possibilities by the Universe itself."

"Later I learned Rohit Shetty was still undecided and he stayed in the building. He will stay there until he decides. There were others who decided as per their choices."

"I decided to jump out from the building's balcony and remain in the same universe."

Riya Kundu and Rakesh Prakash were listening patiently.

Riya Kundu spoke, *"Some laws of the universe should never be broken!"*

Raghu Dayal continued speaking, *"You know Riya, I have come to realise that there are no laws in this universe."*

"*Laws are created to tame a developed mind. You can create as many laws as possible. You can create any law you want and if you are able to convince enough people it becomes the law of the universe. But at the same time, if even one person believes in anything else, he will have a different universe created with his own set of laws. This is how parallel universes exist at the same time within the same space time. This is the truth and there is nothing more complex here.*"

"*Remember we considered earth to be flat just a few centuries back. There was nothing wrong with this fact or believing in it. And if you were born during that time you would consider that as a universal law. We can start believing again that the earth is flat and if there are enough believers again, the earth will become flat again for all of us.*"

"*This is the power of the conscious mind which will evolve forever. You or your organisation cannot stop and tame its growth by feeding your own ideas and versions of your ideas to the Universal Mind.*"

Riya Kundu looked uninfluenced by what Raghu Dayal had to say. It seemed like she has heard all this rebellious talk beforehand.

"*I had enough of your gibberish, Raghu. My duty is to protect the Universe as it is now. 'The Ancients' have trust in me and I cannot break the trust.*"

"*I have killed you once and I am going to do that again. This time I am going to make sure that your mind is lost as well.*"

"And for your information G Reddy choose to jump out of the building as well. He was severely ill out of chronic disease. Guruji has to put his son down to release him of his agony. We will sacrifice anyone for our cause."

Rakesh Prakash was visibly shocked to hear all this revelations.

Raghu Dayal hearing this was agitated for the first time since they met him. He said in a stern voice.

"Riya Kundu! You did not get it at all. The development of human mind is a natural progression. If I can do it with a bit of discipline, concentration and meditation, any one can."

"The secret about the infinite power and possibilities of human mind cannot be part of the secret of a select few in your organisation."

"This is a revolution for unleashing the powerful mind which is going on now. This is the next milestone in the development of the universe."

"Neither you nor your organisation can stop this!"

But Riya Kundu was on a mission. She had enough of it from Raghu Dayal now.

"Shoot!"

There was a loud sound from her revolver.

The trigger has been pressed.

And there was Raghu Dayal lying dead on the floor of his own hut.

Riya Kundu looked at Rakesh Prakash who looked quite disturbed.

"Don't worry Rakesh! I will not harm you. You have been very useful to us in finding the three of them and helping put them down to peace."

Then she shouted, *"Hey look back, there's G Reddy."*

As he looked back, Riya Kundu jumped towards Rakesh Prakash and hit him hard on his head with the revolver. He lay there unconscious.

Just then Riya Kundu's mobile started ringing.

She smiled and informed the person on the phone, *"Yes, the ordeal is finally over. Order has been restored."*

CHAPTER 25

Exactly a year after this incident, a little boy was walking with her mother towards the 'Shani Mandir'.

He shouted with excitement.

"Mamma, what is that old building doing here? I have never seen it here before!"

"Ya son, I have never seen it there either."

Suddenly the front gate of the apartment opened.

Rohit Shetty was walking out. He looked in a much better shape now. He was more calm and composed.

Once outside the old haunted building he shouted, *"World! I am back."*

The boy took his water bottle and walked towards Rohit Shetty.

"Uncle, here is the water you asked from me right now."

The boy's mother looked puzzled because she did not hear anything.

Rohit Shetty winked at the boy and walked away in style.